SAVAGE'S
salvation

HURRICANE HEAT MC BOOK 3

www.chellebliss.com

USA TODAY BESTSELLING AUTHOR

This is a work of fiction. Names, characters, places, and incidents either are the product of the author's imagination or are used fictitiously, and any resemblance to actual persons, living or dead, business establishments, events, or locales is entirely coincidental. The publisher does not assume any responsibility for third-party websites or their content.

All Rights Reserved. No part of this book may be reproduced, scanned, or distributed in any printed or electronic format without permission.

Publisher © Bliss Ink February 26th 2026
Edited by Silently Correcting Your Grammar
Proofread by Read By Rose & Shelley Charlton
Cover Design © Chelle Bliss
Cover Photo © Wander Aguiar

Hurricane Heat MC Series

Book 1 - Shadow's Protection
Book 2 - Phantom's Healing
Book 3 - Savage's Salvation
Book 4 - Hawk's Hope
... and more to come

Please visit *menofinked.com/hurricane* for the latest series information.

ONE
SAVAGE

I FUCKING HATE SURPRISES. And when I roll up to the abandoned warehouse with Shadow and Phantom, the last thing I want to be is surprised. But here we fucking go.

We idle our bikes a safe distance down a sun-faded and cracked asphalt drive.

"Hold up." I raise a hand and look over the rims of my sunglasses. The Florida sun is blasting my eyes, but I can still make out the shape of a man a thousand feet away who is *not* the contact we're here to do business with. Even at this distance, I can see long, scraggly gray hair peeking out of a filthy, salt-stained cowboy hat. I lift my chin to Phantom, President of Hurricane Heat, whose bike idles a few feet away from mine. "I know Anthony," I say. "And that ain't him."

Just like my legal given name ain't Savage, I'm sure the guy who's been on the other end of the secure chats I've had over the last three months isn't really

"Anthony" either. I don't give a shit if he calls himself Santa Fucking Claus. As long as he shows up and does the deal like we've been planning, we're good. But my contact isn't here, and that means we are far from good right now.

Phantom can't see my eyes behind my shades, but I'm glaring and reaching a hand to tap the reassuring shape of the gun I have secured at my waist. We're here to buy more weapons, but I suddenly wish I'd packed much more firepower.

Phantom pinches the bridge of his nose with two fingers, curses, pulls his phone out of his back pocket, and taps out a furious text.

Then, we wait.

The heat of the summer afternoon is oppressive, and I'm already way past irritable. The sun beats hard on the back of my neck, and I grab a red paisley bandana from my back pocket to mop up the thick, salty droplets before they soak their way down my back. The three of us are dressed in our leathers, the vests identifying us as the executive branch of the Heat. Phantom is the president, Shadow is the VP, and I'm the sergeant-at-arms. Having the three of us here is a show of force, but also a sign of good faith.

If all three of us go down in a bad deal, the stability of the entire club would topple. Not that my brothers wouldn't pick up the pieces fast. I know they would. We've lost members and had to regroup from more shit than I care to remember in the twelve years I've been part of this club.

What pisses me off and sets my blood boiling hotter than my neck under this damned sun is the fact that these assholes aren't showing us the respect we're showing them.

I squint and make out a pickup truck parked alongside three bikes near the entrance to the warehouse. The truck's a real piece of shit. Rusted, faded orange that once was red back when anybody gave a shit about the thing. Anyone or anything could be planted in that truck. Even though I'm more than a decade out of the service, my training and instincts kick in. This has ambush written all over it, and I'm not putting my brothers in the line of fire, no matter how big this deal is. "Fuck this," I say, revving my engine. "I say we roll."

Phantom holds up a finger. "Let me deal with this."

He gets off his bike, and both Shadow and I hover our hands over our weapons. We've got Viper in a truck idling half a mile away, but if anything goes down, it'll be just the three of us to who knows how many there are of them.

"Let me go talk to them," I say. "I'll find out where the prick is."

Phantom doesn't have to say a word. He just shakes his head, and I stand down. Mad Dog is the president of the Hellfires. If he's out front, then Phantom's got to meet him with equal respect. I'm tense as a dog about to enter a fight as I watch Phantom walk the long, weathered driveway, stick out his hand, and talk with the Hellfires crew. I don't let my eyes leave Phantom, my fingers itching to pull out my gun, but every once in a while, I track movement in the pickup truck that sets my palms itching. I don't like this one bit, and my blood pressure is rising faster than the temperature of the asphalt.

When Phantom turns his back to the Hellfires crew and makes a leisurely walk back toward us, I squint through my sunglasses and watch for the slightest movement from the direction of the warehouse. I need one wrong move—one ass-scratch that makes me feel off—and I'll start shooting. Anything to protect my brothers.

But Phantom seems unbothered as he walks up to Shadow and me.

"What the fuck?" I demand. "Where's my guy?"

"Anthony's got bigger problems than this." Phantom sighs. "He's dead."

My jaw nearly drops open. "Dead? What the fuck? I just talked to him last week."

Phantom shrugs. "Happened three days ago, if Mad Dog ain't lyin'."

"And if he is?" Shadow's gray T-shirt is soaked with sweat. He shifts uncomfortably on his bike and shakes his head. "You trust this guy?"

"No. I don't." Phantom holds up his phone. He shoots off a text. "I told Mad Dog, under the circumstances, we're gonna take a minute to discuss the change in personnel."

Shadow chuckles at Phantom's use of the word

personnel, but I can't crack a grin. This was my deal. My contact. And like I said, I don't like surprises.

We sweat like pigs and wipe our faces while we wait for Phantom to get the text back he's waiting for. It comes within about two minutes, which seem to stretch on like two hours. He finally gets an answer, reads the text, and raises a brow.

"My contact in the sheriff's office confirmed it. Accident up on Route 90. It's still under investigation, so nothing's been released to the public. But the guy you know as Anthony is dead."

I drop more f-bombs than sweat droplets. "Why the fuck didn't somebody contact me?"

But I know the answer to that. It's a stupid question that I spit out because I'm fucking pissed off. Most of us use secure apps on our phones, apps that don't back up messages or photos to any kind of cloud storage. If Anthony had his device on him when he went down, the device is probably gone. And with it, all the messages we'd sent. The only way the Hellfires would know how to contact me is by showing up to do the deal.

And this is a big deal.

Viper's in a truck with a bag of cash about a half mile away, waiting for our signal. The Hellfires are the only club in Florida that can get what we need at a cost that won't make our asses bleed. I can see why, with that kind of cash on the line, nobody risked scaring us off by getting in touch. Showing up today was about the only option they had under the circumstances. Still, I don't like it. I don't like how it looks, feels, or smells.

"We in or we out?" The question comes from Shadow. He's looking from my face to Phantom's, no doubt trying to figure out whether my skeptical side or Phantom's practical side is going to win out.

"We need that product," Phantom says. "And they have it on lock. If we walk now…" He shakes his head.

I clench my hands into fists. If I second-guess Phantom's call, I'm second-guessing the man himself. I trust my brothers with my life. I don't like any of this, but if Phantom's in, I'm not going to insult him by backing out.

"New plan," I say. "I want to run surveillance." I want eyes on everything that happens. Every movement these assholes make. I trust my hand, my weapon, and my finger on the trigger to protect my brothers.

"Done." Phantom nods at Shadow, and they walk together toward the front of the warehouse.

I follow behind, scanning the perimeter. I swallow against the dryness in my throat, wishing like hell I had time to drink the water I stowed on my bike. But as soon as we reach the warehouse door, I forget the sticky heat and laser-focus on the man with the teeth and the filthy cowboy hat.

"You Savage?" He's looking at me, his arms tanned as leather and covered in prison-style faded tattoos.

I nod but don't say anything else.

"I'm your new contact now." The name on his patch

reads Mad Dog, and he sure as hell looks like one. Thick, scraggly whiskers graze the collar of his white wifebeater tank. His nasty gray curls are tied back in a low ponytail under the cowboy hat. He extends a hand to me, and I just look at it while he introduces himself.

"Mad Dog."

I nod again, not happy about this little meet-cute, but I extend my hand. "Sorry to hear about Anthony."

Mad Dog snarls, but he doesn't say any actual words. Then he turns to Phantom and motions him inside.

Savage and I trade looks.

This is the part I hate most. We're not going to do this kind of a deal out in the open, so the level of trust that's required at this stage in the negotiation makes the ulcer I've been fighting for the better part of my life turn my gut into a volcano. My stomach twists as I watch my brothers follow Mad Dog and two of his flunkies inside a warehouse where anything—and anyone—could be waiting. Cops. Feds. More assholes looking to shake us down and take us out.

I hold the air in my lungs until my chest burns and I'm literally pouring sweat, pacing outside the front of the building. I fire off a text to Viper to let him know Shadow and Phantom are inside, and then I set my sights on the faded pickup.

I've seen movement through the grime-coated windows but haven't heard any sound. If things go to plan, the conversation inside that warehouse should last ten minutes, tops. Then Viper will roll in around the back with the cash, we'll load the truck with guns, and we'll get the fuck out of the Hellfires territory.

This isn't the first deal we've done with them, but the location and the players always change.

The Hellfires ain't like the Heat.

They're ruthless, and they live up to their reputation. The Heat ain't saints by any stretch, but we prefer to dabble in easy money and low body-count jobs. We'll move drugs and money, but we don't take people out unless we have to protect our own, and we don't traffic humans. Dealing with this club is a necessary evil, part of the job. If we want to do what we do, we need what they sell, and they're the best way to get what we need.

But that doesn't mean I don't hate doing deals with the devil.

I scan the perimeter of dead grass, overgrown weeds, and discarded trash. A shithole lot with a shithole warehouse, but the sight lines are long. Unless the Hellfires have guys down in the long grass, there's nobody out here. I take a shaky breath and check my watch.

Times like these, I wonder what my other "brothers" are up to. I used to be a very different man. I'm sure some of the guys from my unit are overseas. Some are retired. Some didn't survive their deployments. And then there's me. Out here playing soldier in a leather vest with illegal guns in the wilds of Florida.

But I don't have time for regrets. Not when I notice a sudden movement inside the truck that sets my teeth on edge. I check my watch again. Phantom and Shadow walked into that warehouse three minutes ago. I've got more than enough time to check out whoever the hell is playing lookout in that truck.

I approach from the rear, walking so fast my boots echo against the hot asphalt. The window on the driver's side door is open a crack, and I'm about to pound my fist against the door when I see a brown bun —messy and knotted on the top of someone's head. I squint through the crack in the window, but I can't see shit.

I pound on the door. "Hey," I call out. "Who's inside?"

The person in the truck moves so fast it's like she's been tased. She peers at me through the crack in the window, and I can make out one brown eye and one enormous purple shiner.

It's a woman and she's hurt.

"Hey." I rap gently on the window. "Open the door."

The woman trembles and doesn't say a word.

I lean a little closer to the window and see that her face is flushed bright red and droplets of sweat trickle down the sides of her face.

"Hey," I say again. "It's too hot for you to be in there with the window closed. Open the door. Let in some fresh air. I'm not going to bother you."

She rolls down the window—a slow, cranking motion—another inch, though, and my stomach turns over. The black eye looks fresh.

I don't want to scare her, and fuck knows I don't want to get involved in whatever this is. A tiny part of me hears alarm bells blasting through my memory banks at all the black eyes I grew up watching my mom cover with layer after layer of makeup. The way she looked at me, her head low, reminds me of what this girl is doing right now.

"What's your name?" I ask cautiously, shoving aside the memories.

She won't respond. Doesn't even acknowledge that I spoke.

"Listen," I say, my heart at war with my head. I should not get involved. The last time I got between a woman and the shit-for-brains who beat her…it cost me everything. My career, my family. My future. Whatever this is, I don't need to get any closer than I am.

But then I hear a whimper. That's when I almost fucking lose it.

"Do you have a baby in there with you? Open the door and let in a little fresh air. You two have got to be hot. I promise I'm not going to hurt you."

I take ten steps back and hold my hands up in front of me. "Go on now. Open the door."

She blinks at me through the window, and I wince at the way her swollen lid tries to close.

Fuck. Fuck. Fuck, that looks like it hurts, and my ulcer bubbles up pure acid at the thought of what she's going through right now.

Her face disappears, but then, slowly and carefully, the driver's side door creaks open. No wonder she didn't want to open it. If she's hiding out from whoever gave her the beating, that loud-ass door is like a siren.

When the door opens a crack, I wave at her in greeting. "Can I come a little closer? I have water in my bike if you need some."

She looks away from me but shakes her head slightly. "No," she whispers but then repeats it a little louder. "No water. Thanks, though."

I take one step closer to the truck. "Hey, what's your name?" I ask again, gently this time. But then I'm at a loss. She's got to know what we're doing here.

I draw in a deep breath and try to shove the memories away. This woman is not my problem.

Not my problem.

Not my problem.

"I'm Claire," she says softly, as if just by knowing her name, I have the power to hurt her. And God, she doesn't need more of that. "And, uh, this," she says, her eyes never leaving mine, "is Aurora."

She nods a little, and I take a few more steps toward the truck. I stand a safe distance away, but I can see through the crack in the door that she's holding a sleeping baby in her arms. No wonder she's hot. The baby's silky brown hair looks wet and stuck to her little head. The kid's feet are bare, and she's wearing just a little T-shirt and a diaper that, from the looks of it, desperately needs changing.

Claire doesn't look so good herself. Her messy brown bun is matted and tangled, and the shorts and tank top she has on look like she's been wearing them for a couple of days—at least. Claire is skinny—too skinny—for somebody who's got a little baby. To make things worse, the arm that clutches her daughter is covered in faded, hand-sized yellow marks.

I'm simultaneously nauseated and infuriated, and everything comes rushing out of me at once. "Are you with them?" I ask, my question coming out angrier than I intend. "You with Mad Dog?"

She bites her lower lip and shakes her head. "No… no. He's my ex's half brother. My ex…died…a couple days ago. I have no place else to go, so Mad Dog is…"

She swallows, and her eyes flutter shut. I don't know what that means, what Mad Dog has been doing to her, but then it hits me.

"Anthony?" I ask. "Your baby's daddy is—was —Anthony?"

She nods, but there's something strange in her face when I say his name. She doesn't look like a devastated widow. And I start to wonder if maybe that black eye is about three days old…

Just then, the sound of tires on asphalt distracts me from the conversation, and Claire slams the truck door closed like the devil himself is after her.

I look up and see Viper give me a wave as he pulls around the back of the warehouse. I check my phone. I have a text from Phantom giving the all clear. Viper's going out back to get the product and to hand off the money.

The deal's almost done.

I jog back to my bike and grab the unopened bottle

of water that I'm glad I didn't bother drinking. I go back to the truck and open the door, handing the bottle to Claire. "It's not open," I tell her. "Take it. I brought it for me. It's hot as the devil's dick out here. Keep yourself hydrated."

She makes no move to take it, but I keep my hand out, trying not to stare at the vicious black eye. Jesus Christ. I can't handle this right now. I shove the bottle at her and close the truck door behind me just as Phantom and Shadow leave the warehouse. Phantom nods at me.

Phantom, Shadow, Mad Dog, and I all exchange handshakes, and then we wait until Viper rolls up and idles the truck on the driveway, the transaction finally concluded. Viper waits while we walk back to our bikes. I'm halfway down the asphalt drive when I hear the ear-shredding creak of the shitty truck door opening.

"Get the fuck out of there." I hear Mad Dog's voice, low and mean, and despite the sweltering temperature, my blood runs cold.

I turn back and see that shady cowboy wannabe yank Claire out of the truck by the arm that's not holding tight to her baby girl. Claire flinches like she's ready to dodge another blow to the face, and she stumbles on bare feet.

Mad Dog is practically dragging her away from the truck when I stop in my tracks.

"Savage?" Phantom's voice is low. He knows my history. Knows the highs and lows, the failure, and who I blame for everything. "What's going down?"

I don't say anything. I just turn to him and say, "I got to do this." I don't wait for a response. I storm across the asphalt, trying not to imagine the soles of this woman's feet burning while I've got inches of leather between me and the road. "Hey!" I shout after Mad Dog, trying my best to swallow every insult my furious brain can conjure up.

"You forget somethin'?" Mad Dog doesn't even bother to loosen his hold on Claire. He cocks his head at me and flares his nostrils, daring me to say something.

"How much for the girl?" I ask him. "And the baby."

Mad Dog cocks a brow at me and looks from her back to me. "You see something you like?" he asks.

"All I want to know is what you want for her," I say. "All in. No strings, no contact. All mine."

His face drops, and he spits on the ground. He names a price—not even half what we paid for the guns. "Add in another five Gs, and you can have the truck too."

I look back at Phantom, who's looking at me like I've lost my damn mind. I may have, but I've gone too far now.

"Blade's going to shit his pants," Phantom says low under his breath.

I know that. Our club treasurer acts like he's the chair of the Federal Reserve. He manages our money so we can make "investments" like this one—buying weapons—and makes sure we always have more than enough in reserve. The club supports a lot of people, and our numbers are growing. That means our businesses need to grow too. This transaction, though, isn't going to make a dent in the club kitty. This is a personal debt.

I pull out my phone and text my lawyer. I have the money, and my lawyer knows how to get at it. This is my choice. "My money," I mutter to Phantom. I don't want Mad Dog overhearing anything that could make him change his mind or up his price. It's already steep enough to do some real damage. "This is on me, not the club," I tell Phantom, ignoring the look on his face. Then I turn back to Mad Dog.

"Cash'll be here in thirty minutes," I tell him. "But you can keep your shit truck."

I point to Claire, so she knows what's about to go down. "You got anything you need to grab?" I know the answer before she says it. But she doesn't even speak. Her undamaged eye is wide and red, like she's fighting back tears.

I try to soften my voice so I don't scare her, but I don't want to give Mad Dog or anyone else a reason to look too closely. "Get in that truck. The driver'll put the AC on. You got a kiddie seat for her?"

Claire again shakes her head, and I do my best not to give Mad Dog a punch that'll make him wish he had Claire's injuries instead of the ones I want to give him.

"Go. Get in the truck and stay cool," I growl. "It's too hot out here for a baby with no water."

Mad Dog roughly shoves her away, and with help from Shadow, Claire stumbles over the dry, dead grass and climbs into the truck. I follow her and lean in to talk to Viper.

"Get out of here as soon as the money arrives," I tell Viper. "Put the AC on. These two are fucking cooking."

Viper looks at me as though I've lost my damned mind, and maybe I have. I can't think about it now. I've got to focus on finishing what I started and making sure the snakes of the Hellfires don't try to double-cross me before I get this woman to safety. What the hell I'll do with her then...I have no fucking clue.

Phantom, Shadow, and I don't talk while we wait for the sleek black car to pull onto the driveway. Finally, a man in a three-piece suit climbs out. I greet him, shaking his hand, while never taking my eyes off Mad Dog. After talking with me quietly, the guy hands me a lockbox. I give Mad Dog the box that contains his money and the passcode to unlock it. After he opens it and counts the cash, he whistles through his shitty teeth.

"If I'd known she was worth so much, I'd have sold her a hell of a long time ago." Then he turns and signals to his crew to roll out. "Nice doing business with you boys."

The Heat waits until both Mad Dog's crew and my drop-off guy have left before we roll.

"You know what the fuck you're doing?" Phantom asks, lowering his sunglasses over his eyes. I don't need to see his expression to know what he's thinking.

I'm thinking the same damn thing, and I say it out loud.

"I don't have the slightest idea what I just did," I admit.

Phantom lets out a deep sigh. "A baby, a woman... Fuckin' nuts, brother."

When he says that, the implications of what I did hit me. Phantom flares his nostrils and rubs his eyes hard, shoving his thumbs under his sunglasses. We stay there for a minute as the reality sort of sinks in. We're about to put up a baby and a woman at the compound. I know nothing about her, other than what I can see.

And now, she's completely my problem.

What I'm thinking must be written all over my face because Phantom waves a hand at me and sighs. "It's fucking done, so we deal with it. I'll put in a call to Poppy. Let her know we're going to have guests."

Poppy is Phantom's old lady. Between them, they have three kids and another on the way. Poppy'll know what to do once Claire gets to the compound. But me...I don't know the first thing about taking care of someone, let alone providing for a baby.

The enormity of it hits me, and I look over to Viper's truck. I see the top of Claire's hair, the rat's nest of a bun on her head the only thing that's visible. She must be slouched down out of sight, holding her baby.

The image of her hiding back there, barefoot, vulnerable, and most definitely hurt, sets my brain back to balance. No matter what I'm worried about, her fears have got to be through the roof. She just got passed off from the Hellfires to the Heat.

Talk about out of the frying pan and into the fire.

She has no way of knowing she's safe now. That her nightmare is over—if she wants it to be.

Maybe we'll get her out of here and she'll run off, and I can rest easy knowing that I did what I could when I had the chance. Who the hell knows…

For a guy who hates surprises, this day has been full of them. And I have a feeling this is only the beginning.

TWO
CLAIRE

I USED to be good at things. I used to have a job, a home. Friends and a social life. I used to have beautiful clothes and cared how I looked when I left the house.

But now, sitting in the back seat of this truck, my sweaty thighs stuck to the leather, behind a man who looks as mean as a young Mad Dog—whose name I don't know, who is taking me and my daughter God only knows where… I can't believe there was ever a time I was anything other than what I am now.

Broke.
Broken.
Bought.

How did I get to this place in my life? I mean, I know the story. I know the guy I fell for, the way he changed, the ways I failed to see so many signs before it was too late.

But now? I'm literally powerless.

I have a driver's license in my back pocket and my

baby in my arms. That's it. I have the signs all over my face and body, showing what it cost for us just to make it out alive.

I guess that has to mean something.

We're alive. We're together.

What happens next... We'll have to just take it as it comes, no matter how scary.

No matter how much worse it gets. But it can't get worse... Can it?

Famous last words that I vow to never, ever say again.

Aurora is sound asleep. The guy driving the pickup sounds impatient, and I can't imagine the world of hurt we'd be in if she were fussing.

"There's a blanket back there," he barks. "I'll turn up the AC. Cover that baby and stay low. I'm going to drive nice and easy." He says baby like it puts a sour taste in his mouth, but that doesn't surprise me. The guys of the Hellfires club weren't exactly fans of my daughter either.

I close my eyes and rest my head against the back of the seat, trying to disappear into the chilled leather.

I must have fallen asleep in the first cool air I've felt all day, my baby tucked against me, because the next thing I know, the truck is slowing to a stop. The guy behind the wheel turns in his seat. "Stay here. Someone'll come for you."

I'm shocked that I dozed off, and I feel a little sick waking up. It takes me a minute to remember where we are and what happened before my stomach sinks.

Someone is coming to get me.

My mind races through the possibilities, each one worse than the last. Selling me again. Selling my daughter. Keeping us and… My God.

I tighten my hold on Aurora and kiss her sweaty head. No matter what happens, I will go to my grave fighting for this baby. No one has ever laid a hand on my daughter, and the only way anyone is going to hurt her is if my cold, dead corpse is buried six feet deep.

She is all I have, and she is all that matters.

No matter what these people intend, I'll do anything —and I mean anything—to keep my daughter safe.

As soon as the driver leaves the vehicle, I weigh my options. And surprise, surprise, I have none. I could run —but how far would I get barefoot and carrying an infant?

I don't know where I am or what's going to happen to me now that I'm here, but I sure as hell can't make any decisions until I know what they expect of me. I try not to think of my mother, but I can hear her voice in my ear telling me to fight like hell, run like mad, do whatever it takes.

Mom wouldn't believe it if she knew how my life had gone downhill since she passed.

I blink back tears and thank the heavens Momma isn't here to see me fall apart. To watch me let my daughter down in ways that she could so easily have done with me. But my mother was different. She was talented and free. She raised me alone like it was easy, even though I know, behind closed doors, she suffered and struggled. She just never fell this low.

If I were half the woman she was, I would have left Anthony the moment I got pregnant. But I believed his lies. I naïvely hoped... Well, it doesn't matter what I hoped. I tell myself I am strong enough to do whatever it takes. Even if I hardly believe it.

"Are you Claire?"

A woman's voice breaks me out of my thoughts. I lift my head from the cushioned bench seat and see a stunning woman. She looks a little older than me, but her smile is warm and inviting. Just seeing her makes me nearly light-headed with shame. Her long brown hair is styled in beachy waves that fall past her shoulders. She's wearing a little bit of glittery eye shadow and gloss on her full lips, and her nails are painted a pale, summery pink. I know that because her hand hovers over a very pregnant belly.

A pregnant woman? What the hell are these guys into? I didn't think anything could be worse than Anthony and the Hellfires club, but this woman looks amazing. There's no way she's here against her will... Is she?

I must look confused as hell because the woman's face practically melts as she opens the door a little wider. Her eyes land on my daughter, and I instinctively clutch Aurora tighter. She will not take my child. She will not hurt my baby, no matter how pretty she smells.

But the woman makes no move toward us at all. She

just smiles again, beams of literal sunshine streaming from her bright teeth, and she waves. "Oh, hi there, sweetheart."

She babbles away like we're meeting at a summer barbecue and not like I've just been bought off some bikers in an arms deal. "Is that your baby?" she asks. "What is she...six months?"

I nod and swallow down a whole encyclopedia of emotions: fear, dread, and, worst of all, shame. I try not to think of what my filthy feet and matted hair must look like to this woman. Her kindness is setting me a tiny bit at ease—not that I trust her. She must have kids of her own, though. She figured out Aurora's age to the day. Aurora just turned six months last week.

Right before Anthony...

"Your little one must be hungry or at least thirsty." The woman gives me another one of those smiles that is so bright and welcoming, I almost feel a little better. She seems sincere, but I need to be wary.

No one is ever what they seem.

At least, not in my world.

"I'm Poppy, Phantom's wife." She pats her belly, affectionately rubbing a hand over the expensive-looking floral maternity dress. "I have a son, he has two daughters, but this little butterbean is our first together."

I process what she's saying. "I don't know who Phantom is," I mumble, instinctively reaching down to smooth Aurora's hair. I catch a whiff of a sour smell and realize she needs a diaper change.

Poppy grins. "I would say he's the mean-looking one, but they all look pretty scary at first." Her face darkens a little as she looks over my black eye.

To me, these men don't just look mean, they're fucking cruel. The shame rises up yet again, and my throat burns.

She rushes on. "Phantom is the president of the club, the Hurricane Heat. He's that one."

She points to the trio of motorcycles that are pulling up beside the truck. One man, a dark beard covering his face and dark tattoos covering his arms, gets off his bike and heads toward us. I shrink down a little lower in my seat without even realizing I'm doing it. There's no hiding, though. Nowhere in this pickup truck to bury myself and pretend none of this is happening.

As much as I want to melt away and disappear, it's obvious by now that's not happening. If I could go invisible at will, I would have done it years ago.

"You know, honey, it's going to be okay," Poppy says softly to me. "You're completely safe here." She turns then, and a massive set of arms circles her. A man holds her close and murmurs in her ear before giving her a long, passionate kiss on the mouth. His hands snake down to cup her rear end through the light, flowy dress she's wearing, and for a minute, my heart shatters into so many pieces, I don't know how I'll ever pick myself back up.

Anthony never held me like that. Kissed me, treasured me. At first, he showered me with attention. He was intense and demanding, but never like this.

Poppy laughs and lifts on her toes, and I can see she's wearing the cutest sandals. She's beauty, light, and joy, and she's a mother with another on the way.

"Claire, is it?" Phantom has let Poppy go, and he's bending down to peer into the back seat. "Poppy's going to take good care of you." He slaps her behind, and she shakes her head then gives him another kiss before he walks back to his bike.

Poppy gives me a huge grin and waves her beautiful, tanned, slim arms. "Come on," she says. "Let's get you settled."

Settled? I don't know what that means. Who these people are. What they think of me, what they want from me. In that moment, I can't believe that I feel worse being around pretty people, people who love and care for each other, than I did being trapped with Mad Dog, Anthony, and the Hellfires club.

I can't say anything, and I can't move.

It's all too much, and it hits me all at once, like a freight train to the chest. I look down at what's left of the months-old polish and the dirt and grime from being forced out of the compound barefoot this morning. I feel sick to my stomach.

"Are you okay? You look pale, honey... Savage!" Poppy turns, and all I hear is white noise in my ears, a sudden ringing.

I rest my head back against the seat. I don't know who Savage is, and I don't have the strength to care. The truck is off and the AC has stopped blowing, so the temperature is rising.

"Hey." The guy who *bought* me from Mad Dog climbs into the back of the truck with me and slides across the seat. He stays a good distance away from me, like I'm a wild, caged animal. "Claire?"

He looks me in the eye, and for the first time, I notice how beautiful he is. Not picture-perfect like an actor, but he's rugged. His deep brown eyes meet mine, and the next thing I know, he's nodding at me, holding out his arms.

"Take my hand," he says. "I'm going to get you and your baby out of this truck. We're going to take it nice and slow. Get you food, a shower, and some rest."

I must bristle at the word shower... I need one so badly, but... What will they expect from me in return? I shake my head. "I don't want to. I don't want to go with you."

"Claire." His voice is so soft and low. "I'm going to say this as many times as you need to hear it, so listen good. You're safe here. You and your baby are safe. Nobody's going to hurt you here. We're going to help you get on your feet. You don't have to worry about anything but getting your strength back."

I don't know how he knows I'm weak. I must look as bad as I feel. I don't even want to think how I look to them. I only know for sure how bad I feel.

"Claire," he says again, and his voice is so gentle. "No one here is going to hurt you. I'm not going to let anything happen to you for as long as you're under our roof. Do you understand?"

I lift my head slowly, but I can't speak. I can't

believe what he says. I can't dare to trust that maybe, maybe, he's telling the truth. Luck doesn't happen to people like me.

I used to believe in luck and happy endings. I used to laugh and feel beautiful, but that was a long time ago.

He holds out a hand to me. "Come with me," he says. "Get out of the truck. Let's go inside. You'll have a room just for you and the baby."

I look at Poppy. She's standing beside him, and I notice she's leaning forward, her beautiful, soft curls framing her face like an angel. She's resting a hand on his shoulder and nodding. "You look like you're going to faint, honey," she says gently. "You need food and some water. Let us help you."

I swallow a wave of nausea and allow their words to sink in. I can't stay stuck to this seat forever, and both my daughter and I will need a place to sleep tonight.

I promise myself I will steal what I need and we will run at the first sign of anything we don't like.

I promise myself I won't make the same mistakes I made with Anthony.

I make myself a promise that we will be okay.

I'm not strong right now, but there is nothing I wouldn't do to protect my daughter. Even if that means doing the thing I cannot fathom ever doing again and trusting someone.

Poppy is smiling so big, I have to look away. When I look at Savage, there is something I can't read in his eyes. He's big and tattooed and mean-looking, for sure.

But there's something else. The same thing I saw when he gave me his water when I was in Mad Dog's truck. The same thing I saw when he watched Mad Dog yank me so hard I almost dropped Aurora.

I don't know what it is I see in him. And I sure don't understand why. But I sit up slowly, hug my baby closer to my chest, and take his hand.

"Follow me," Poppy says, motioning for me to follow her.

I do, but my steps are heavy. This place is a heck of a lot nicer than what the Hellfires call home. But it has the same vibe. Pool table, big TVs, a huge bar. Posters on the walls, recliner chairs and couches that look very comfortable.

There are a lot of people around—guys in jeans and T-shirts, some wearing their leather vests. Some women too. Just like over at the Hellfires' compound. But something about this place feels less desperate and more homey. A woman is standing behind the bar, popping the cap off a bottle of beer and handing it to a guy whose massive back is covered in leather. I make quick eye contact with her, take in her big, fake boobs and her heavily made-up face. I'm braced for her to scowl or curse, but she looks at me and smiles.

I look down at my toes and follow Poppy down a long, narrow hallway. The guy who bought me follows close behind me. Maybe to keep an eye on his investment? Maybe to make sure I don't try to run, pass out, or get sick on their floors? I don't know. My nerves are so fried right now, I can't think straight.

We pass a bunch of closed doors, and my heart sinks. I wonder where they are taking me. What kind of hellhole they'll toss me into. But my throat is dry, and my knees are too weak. I can't run. I can't ask questions. I can't even fight. I feel a sting of tears as I whisper an apology against my daughter's warm head.

How did I fail her so badly?

I follow Poppy wordlessly past door after door until, finally, she pulls a key from a pocket in her dress and unlocks a door.

"So, this room is yours." Poppy waves a perfectly manicured hand around the space. She walks in, and I follow her. "Phantom got this for me as a surprise, but since I don't need it, you can use this until we get you one of your own."

I follow her hand and notice that she's pointing to a crib. An actual crib. With sheets and baby blankets and everything. It's white wood, and it looks brand-new. It's beautiful. Like the crib I would have wanted for my daughter if she'd ever been able to have anything like that. She never has. I can hardly believe what I'm seeing.

I look from Poppy to the crib and back, not able to process what's going on. I say nothing.

Poppy motions toward the closet. "I didn't know your size, but when Phantom called to tell me you were coming, I grabbed a couple things from my closet at home and a few things from the girls here. There's a bunch of sizes, and it's all clean, so wear whatever you feel comfortable in until we can take you shopping."

Take me shopping.

Take me shopping?

I look from her to the man who's lingering just inside the doorway. He hasn't come all the way in, as if he's expecting some kind of invitation.

"I don't understand," I say quietly. "I don't…"

Poppy's grin fades a bit. I can't tell if she's angry or confused, but I brace for her to start screaming.

"Honey," she says gently, "Savage will get you taken care of once you're settled. But for tonight at least, will you mind using what we have here? I'm going to send one of the prospects to pick up diapers and formula. Whatever you need, just let me know. I'll write it all down."

Would I mind? Whatever I need? I have so many questions, I hardly know where to begin. But I ask the one I need to know the answer to the most. "Who is Savage?" I ask cautiously.

Poppy laughs. She jerks a thumb at the man in the doorway. "That's him right there."

Of course. The guy who bought me.

I nod. "And is this your room?" I look from the plain gray sheets to the light blankets on the bed. There are no personal items in this room. No photos or anything. A small couch, the crib, a double bed, and a dresser. It looks like there is a small closet, and then there's another door. Maybe that one connects to his room? Because this room sure doesn't look lived-in.

Savage grunts and shakes his head. "My room's down the hall. When I stay here at the compound, at least. This is a spare room for you and the baby. You'll have total privacy at all times."

Poppy holds up a key. "This locks the door from the outside. Phantom has a copy, but only in case of emergencies. It's in a lockbox in his office. When you and your daughter are inside, you can lock the dead bolt. And when you leave, you can lock the door, but you really don't have to." She laughs. "I can't imagine these guys breaking in for diapers."

"If they've had enough to drink, I wouldn't put anything past 'em." Savage chuckles, but then, looking at me, he shakes his head. "You don't need to worry," he tells me. "They'll keep it chill while you're here."

Poppy laughs again. "Before we moved in together, Phantom's daughters would stay here all the time. A lot of the guys have girlfriends or kids. They know how to behave when there are kids around."

She walks across the room and opens a small door. "Your room has a private bathroom, and I grabbed a couple of toiletries and some soap, but of course you're going to need a lot more." She pulls a cell phone out of her pocket and opens an app. "I'll make a list. What size diapers does your daughter need? Any food allergies? What brand of food does she like?"

Poppy rattles off so many questions, and I can't

answer any of them. I mumble answers, embarrassed to admit the truth.

Aurora eats whatever is cheapest. Whatever Anthony felt like picking up at the dollar store or the discount grocery mart.

What are they going to want from me in exchange for all of this? I can't think about that now.

All I can do is take it one minute at a time.

Aurora starts fussing, and my whole brain shuts off to what's around me. All that matters is my little girl.

"Hey, baby," I coo, bouncing her lightly, her very wet diaper sloshing under my arms.

"Oh my God." Poppy's voice is soft and so reverent. She ducks her head, and her brows come together like she wants to cry. "Those are the most beautiful blue eyes I've ever seen. Look at you, angel." She doesn't move toward us, but a sheen of tears comes into her eyes. "What's her name?"

"Aurora," a deep voice says.

I don't say it. The man in the doorway remembered.

"Aurora." Poppy echoes it, looking back at him, and then turns to me and nods. "My God, she's gorgeous. My daughters are going to flip when they meet her." She looks to me quickly. "I'm not saying you have to let them babysit. They are going to beg, though. They're teenagers—fourteen and seventeen—and they are dying for this baby." She pats her belly. "So, no pressure to let them practice on Aurora."

"Knock-knock." There is another voice at the door. I turn and see the woman from behind the bar resting her chin on Savage's shoulder. She's peeking over him and grinning at us. "Hey, Poppy babe. There's no way I'm letting some prospect make a run for baby shit. I'm going to do it myself. Do Mama and Baby want to come along?"

Poppy looks at me and lifts her brow. "I think Stella's right. You want to come? We'll make a trip out together?"

I swallow hard and look down at myself. I shake my head. I don't want to go, but I also don't really want Poppy to leave me alone. Suddenly, having her nearby feels safe.

As if she can read my thoughts, Poppy shakes her head. "You know what, Stel, why don't you take Savage? There's no bathtub in Claire's bathroom, so maybe she'll want me to help with Aurora while they clean up and get changed."

"Cool. Should we buy a tub, then? Is that a thing? Like a baby pool for inside? I don't know shit about kids." Stella is cracking up, and Poppy laughs with her.

"Get whatever you think she needs." Savage's voice is low. "Get it all."

"I got your list, Poppy. I'm on it." Stella holds up her cell phone, then spins and heads back down the hallway, leaving me alone with Savage and Poppy.

He turns to leave but then stops and looks at Poppy.

"Can I have a minute with Claire?"

Poppy starts to leave, but I shake my head. I don't even mean to. It's like my body is reacting before my brain can process. I don't want to be alone with him.

Not yet. I'm not ready. And even if he makes me pay for saying no to him, I'll deal with it later when I've got some fight back in me. Right now, I'm feeling too fragile. I don't trust myself to fight back, and I sure as hell don't trust him.

Do I trust Poppy? Maybe.

She shoots a look at Savage, and he nods. They had a whole conversation about me, I'm sure, without saying a word.

"It's all good," Savage says. "We'll talk right here."

He comes into the room but stands a healthy distance away from me. He keeps his eyes on Poppy, as if making sure she's close enough to ensure I don't feel threatened by him.

"Hey, listen," he says gently. "You going to be okay? Poppy will stay with you until you settle in."

I nod, avoiding his eyes.

"I meant what I said out here." He walks backward toward the door. "You're completely safe here. Lock up when I leave, and I'll knock when I'm back. You don't want to open this door, you don't, you hear me?"

I can't look at him. But his voice... The way he doesn't sound angry. Doesn't sound mad. He sounds sincere.

If I didn't know better, if I didn't believe it was impossible, I'd think he wants to help me.

I can't process that. I never had a moment's privacy at the Hellfires' compound.

"All right, then." He looks me over, and I look up at him for the first time since I got out of the truck.

My skin tingles, and I'm shaking inside, my belly weak and knees feeling like jelly because for the first time in as long as I can remember, a man is looking at me with something I am sure I recognize. Kindness. There is nothing else there that I can see. Despite the circumstances, he is nothing short of kind.

Then just like that, he gives me a tight smile. He looks at Aurora and says, "Be back soon, kid." And then, he's gone.

My shoulders sag in relief the minute he's gone. But I won't get too comfortable. Because like he said, he'll be back, and then I'll find out what he has planned for me.

THREE
SAVAGE

IF I THOUGHT RESCUING a woman from the Hellfires was expensive, buying shit for a baby makes what I've already spent look like chump change. Stella and I have our arms full as we head back into the club. When we reach the bar, Stella drops her bags.

Blade, our club treasurer, is sitting on a barstool looking a little lost. "Shit day," he says, but he doesn't say more. Blade's a single dad, and though it's been a while since his kid was a baby, I make a mental note to ask him if I run into any issues with Claire and Aurora. No wonder the guy is so tight with the books. A kid—even just one of them—ain't cheap. I clap him on the shoulder.

"Sorry, man," I say to him.

Stella waggles her long fingers, those blood-red nails catching the light.

"I'm off baby duty," she says. "And back on biker duty." She plants a hand on the back of Blade's neck and gives him a friendly, if not slightly flirtatious, massage. "One make-a-shit-day-better neck rub and an ice-cold beer for my Blade coming up." Then she looks back at me. "You got it from here, Savage?"

"Thanks, Stel." I nod, leaving her to fuck around behind the bar.

Plenty of people are filling up the compound now, dinner plates being taken back to the kitchen, TVs blaring, prospects screaming at one another over video games. It's a normal night, except I notice that both Viper and Shadow are gone. I'm sure Viper's handling the product we picked up in the deal today, and Shadow's probably home with his old lady, Violet.

I move to grab the bags that Stella dropped when I feel a hand on my shoulder. Phantom lowers a brow at me, and I know that's him asking for a meeting. The man doesn't use unnecessary words, and anybody in the Heat who's known him for more than five minutes learns how to interpret his grunts. I grab the bags of shit and follow him into his office. Once we're inside, I drop the ridiculous amount of stuff I bought and take a seat.

Phantom leans back against his desk. "You think we're going to have problems?" He gets right into it. "That baby's got a daddy someplace."

I shake my head. "I think it was Anthony, my former contact. If he was taking care of Claire, she might be dead weight now that he's gone. I'm guessing the marks on her face are from him or somebody at the Hellfires who didn't want to have to fund somebody else's old lady." I nod at the overflowing white plastic bags of baby clothes, diapers, food, and even toys. "I think I paid less for my last bike than I spent on this stuff."

Phantom quirks one corner of his mouth. "Don't I fucking know it. That's what's got me worried."

Phantom and Poppy are only about four months away from having a baby of their own. His home is full of shit they've been buying. What's in these bags barely scratches the surface of what that kid's going to need. Not just for tonight or for the next couple of days, but on an ongoing basis. Not to mention Claire herself. The woman came here in a filthy tank top and no shoes. Talk about leaving with the clothes on your back and not a penny to your name.

The reality of that hits me, and I scrub a hand across my face. "Fuck," I mutter.

Phantom nods. "As long as this doesn't become a problem..." He doesn't say more.

I stand and grab the bags. "It'll be my problem if it does." I turn to leave, but he steps forward and stops me with a hand.

"Your problem *is* my problem. It's all of ours," he reminds me. "We're brothers. Just don't keep me in the dark. Something sets off alarm bells, come to me first. I don't want the Hellfires burning a path up to our door."

I understand what he's getting at. I bought Claire's freedom, but that doesn't mean there are no family ties. I remember she said something about Mad Dog being Anthony's half brother. Family is family, and based on what I saw, that would be an explosive family reunion.

"I will," I tell him, but Phantom doesn't release my shoulder.

"I didn't know you had cash like that on hand," he says quietly.

There are parts of my life that I keep private, even from my brothers. I'm not hiding anything, but some things even they don't need to know.

"Saving for retirement," I say lightly, but Phantom just glares at me. I can tell he's worried. But he doesn't need to be. I sock away cash because I have to. I have reasons. Some of the guys here blow every cent they make on booze and bikes. I've got other shit in my life. Shit that no one needs to know about. That money—the money I earn and what I do with it—is the only part of my life that ain't an open book.

A soft knock on the door has me turning.

"Am I interrupting?" Poppy smiles at us.

"Naw, c'mon in, babe." Phantom laces an arm around Poppy's waist, and she rests her head on his shoulder. "How they doin'?" he asks in a low voice.

Poppy looks desperately sad all of a sudden. She looks at me. "That girl, Savage... She's been through hell. I don't know any specifics. She won't talk. Won't open up. Wouldn't even let me hold the baby. She took Aurora into the bathroom with her while she showered. I'm sure she's been doing that since that baby was born." Poppy swallows, and her face flushes red. "It might be the hormones, but God, seeing her like that..." She levels her gaze at me. "That baby looks underweight. I know it's been a long time since I had a little one, but she's so thin and so quiet."

I don't know what any of this means or what I'm supposed to do about it. I look at Poppy and search her face for help.

"I'm sure she's been in survival mode for a long time," she explains. And somehow, that does explain everything. "If you need anything, say the word, okay? I'll bring the girls to help babysit."

I stand up, my stomach sinking with emotion. I can't think about *her*. The other woman in my life, a woman not so different from Claire, and what she went through.

I scratch my head and nod. "Thank you, Poppy. For all you did today. I couldn't have done what you did, and I'm sure she wouldn't have wanted me to be the one to talk to her, get her settled in."

She leaves Phantom and comes close to me. She pulls me into her arms and holds me tightly. I feel the weight and mass of her belly against me, the baby safely protected inside. It's a strange feeling, and it evokes something in me that I don't understand. I wonder if Claire and Aurora have ever felt safe, protected. I try not to think about the pain she has endured and how long she's been tolerating it. I squint my eyes shut and block out my own memories.

When Poppy releases me, she cups my face in her hands and looks me right in the eye. "She's going to need time and space. Go real slow, Savage. Real slow."

I nod. Of course I will. I mean, fuck. I don't know

what I'm doing. I'm not planning on doing anything but dropping off baby shit and backing away. Making sure she gets some sleep. Some food. "She eat?" I ask, suddenly thinking about the sharp collarbones visible through her tank top.

Poppy shakes her head. "No. She had some water, though. Maybe once the baby eats, she will."

"Thank you. Again," I tell her, my words feeling as awkward as I'm sure they sound.

I grab the bags and head down the hallway toward her room, leaving Poppy and Phantom alone. I stand outside Claire's room and listen, but I don't hear a thing. No crying. No talking. No TV. Nothing. I hesitate to knock, but I've got diapers and food the baby probably needs.

"Claire. It's Savage. I've got stuff for the baby." I rap on the door softly with the heel of my hand.

I don't hear anything until the dead bolt flips open. The door opens a crack, and I see Claire's eye—the green one that isn't swollen and marred by bruising.

"I can leave this out here. It's a lot." I set everything down and point to one bag. "This one has the best bottled water. I didn't know there were different kinds of water, but it's heavy. I can bring it in if you want."

She opens the door a crack more. "Okay. You…you can come in."

I shake my head. "It's all right. I don't need to come in, I'll just…"

"Please?" she asks softly. "I have a killer headache,

and it would help me a lot if you'd just bring that in here."

Fuck, fuck, fuck. Of course she does. She hasn't eaten. She has a shitty black eye. I grab the bags and step inside.

I drop the bags right inside the door, which is wide open behind me. Claire is wearing a rock band T-shirt several sizes too big for her over some yoga pants that look like they might belong to one of the girls here. They are loose on her too, emphasizing how thin she is. Her wet hair is wrapped up in a towel, and she's holding Aurora, who is also wrapped in a towel, in her arms.

She looks shyly at the bags. "Did you happen to bring any diapers? I have her in her birthday suit under this towel, and a diaper would be a big help."

I fumble through the bags and grab a purple plastic package with a baby who looks about Aurora's age on it. I hold them out to her. "I can get more tomorrow."

Claire looks at me for a second, studying my face. Then she cracks a tiny smile. "She'll be fine with these for a few days at least. Maybe even a week."

"I don't know how much kids piss and shit," I mutter apologetically. I don't know if I'm ready to find out.

Claire looks at me, her green eyes intently searching my face, and she giggles.

"What?" I ask. "What'd I say?"

She looks away as she gently lays Aurora on the bed

and bends down to carefully reposition the towel so it's under the baby's behind.

"You make babies sound like puppies," she says. "Pissing and shitting…"

I shrug, lifting both my hands in the air. "I don't know," I say. "Isn't that what they do?"

She makes a soft sound as she tears open the diapers. I busy myself taking a bunch of things out of the bags and stacking them neatly on the coffee table. I focus on unwrapping a cheap burner phone I got her, just so she has something to call her family or friends. That feels like a bigger conversation, though, so I take the phone out of the packaging and program in my number.

As I work, I can make out Claire cooing quietly to her daughter, and I hear little noises as she puts the diaper on. Aurora must grab for the towel on her mom's head because I hear a quick intake of breath like Claire is in pain, but then she whispers, "My sweet angel. You're playing with your mama?"

I thought babies screamed and made all kinds of noises, but these two are so, so quiet. Even Aurora's wriggling and sounds while she gets her diaper changed seem too small, too still. A knife twists deep in my chest, and I wonder… Was I like that? Was I trained to stay quiet from my earliest days? Have they spent their entire lifetime like I did, trying to fade away?

Something breaks open in me at the thought, and I have to shatter the silence. I'm not that kid anymore.

And I get to make noise. "You need to eat," I bark, maybe a little too loudly. "I know a great diner."

"I'm done changing her," she says. "You can turn around now."

When I do, I see that Claire's hair is wet and falling over her shoulders. Aurora is holding the towel that was once on her mama's hair in her hands. She's drooling and looking at me with wide, bright, beautiful eyes. Innocent eyes. I swallow the lump in my throat.

"What do you want?" I blurt out.

Claire blinks and bounces lightly on her toes, holding her daughter close. Claire looks so thin and vulnerable, fragile and delicate. The black eye looks even more violent somehow.

"Anything is okay," she says.

I shake my head, emotions churning inside me. Anger—at what she's been through. Fury—that her baby has been through this with her. And rage—all shades of the same color, but each one darker than the next. The uncontrollable side of me, the side I suppress, is raging up like a Florida storm. I've got to focus. Food. Not fists. Not fury. Dinner.

"Claire," I say firmly, dragging my emotions down to a manageable level. "I'm going to go to a diner and get you a nice meal. They have burgers, roast beef, turkey, salads. You a vegan or anything?"

She presses her lips together and shakes her head. "No."

"You like fries? Soup? What do you want?"

She looks scared again. "I don't have..." She glances

down at all the bags. "I don't have money for all this," she says quietly. "For this stuff. For dinner. I have nothing, Savage."

I nod. "I know that. And until you do, I'm taking care of everything. I have money, Claire. And I'm happy to spend it on baby food and diapers and dinner. So, I've just got to know what I'm ordering for you."

She sucks her lower lip into her mouth and cocks her chin at me. "Why?" she asks, her voice a raspy whisper. "Why are you doing this? Because if you…if you expect me… I'm not that." She stands a little straighter, her voice rising. "Anthony was my boyfriend. I wasn't—"

I hold up a hand to silence her, but then I realize she might think I'm threatening her. I shove my hands into my pockets. "I don't care if you're a sex worker, a girlfriend, whatever. No woman, and I mean no woman, deserves to be hurt by anyone, especially not someone she loves."

I realize I'm fisting my hands in my pockets so hard, I'm straining the denim. I try to relax. Think calmer thoughts.

"Someday, we'll talk. But not today. All you need to know right now is I'm helping you because once there was a woman I could not help. I tried." I blink hard and squint against a firestorm of memories. "But I couldn't. I'm helping you now. No questions asked. No debt owed. I have money saved, and I'll help you get on your feet. And I won't expect a goddamn thing in return. You hear me? No one will lay a hand on you for any reason, in any way, while you're under my protection. Are we clear on that?"

She studies my face for a moment, and before dropping down on the bed, her shoulders sag. "I don't understand."

I take the burner phone and toss it onto the bed next to her. "That's for you," I tell her. "You're not a prisoner here. You've got people to call, make the call. You want to leave, the door's wide open. But if you don't, you stay here while you figure out your next move." I point to the phone. "I programmed in my number and Phantom's. He runs this place, so if I'm not available, there are other people who will step in."

She looks at the phone, then at me. The look of doubt on her face is so obvious and clear, I want to reassure her, but I know I can't. She's going to have to learn to trust me. And that shit's going to take time.

"Thank you," she finally says, her voice a meek whimper.

I turn to go, but then I remember. Food. "I'm going to the diner, so tell me what you like or you'll be stuck eating whatever I get."

"Could I have a burger?" I can hardly hear her, but I strain my ears. "And maybe a Coke?"

"Fuck...ahhhh, yes. Heck yes. Definitely a Coke and a burger." I don't know what babies understand, but the hardest part of all this is going to be watching my language. I turn to leave but then realize I didn't ask the most important question. "Claire," I say, one hand on the doorframe. "You want regular or sweet potato fries?"

"Prospect, on your feet." I point at one of the new guys slouched down on a sectional playing video games. "We're making a run."

The other prospects turn and look at us, a little curious and a lot jealous.

The new guy, whose club name is Tank, hoists himself up from the couch. "You got it, boss."

Almost a year ago, we turned over all the prospects we had when one of them named Dylan got himself mixed up in drugs and some drama with Phantom's ex. Since then, we've recruited a bunch of new guys. Some of them, I think, are going to make it. Some won't. Tank's the one I trust the most, and as always, he doesn't ask questions.

Tank's name is fitting. The guy is huge. Shorter than me but wide in every way. He ambles over and tugs a black bandana over his buzz cut. "Who's drivin', boss?"

"Me." I grab a set of keys to a pickup truck from the lockbox on the wall, and we head out to the lot.

I call in an order and add Tank's usual to it. We make the first few minutes of the ride in silence, but eventually, Tank's asking the questions that I am sure are on everyone's minds.

"Lady and a baby, huh?" He stares out the window into the darkness.

I grunt, but then chuckle. "I don't know what the fuck I was thinking." I do, actually, but I'm not about to share that with anyone, let alone a prospect.

Tank's quiet, tapping his fingers lightly on the door, his meaty hand partly out the window. He nods, lost in thought or just respecting the fact that we don't have the kind of relationship that invites him in.

"With an eye like that…" he says quietly. "I hope that I would step in and be a hero like that for someone. I don't know if I would've gotten involved."

I suppose this should be a teachable moment. A moment where I share the club values with this prospect. Tell him what kind of man I am and what kind of person I'd expect him to be. But I'm not that guy. Not anymore. I spent years following orders. Knowing my place. Helping new recruits not get their asses kicked and sometimes doing the ass-kicking. Now, I'm no role model. I'm no leader. I'm just doing what I can to get by without blowing up any more land mines in the landscape of my life.

"We never know who we are until life forces our hand," I say.

He nods because I know he gets it. We all do. I don't have pretty promises or an inspirational slogan. All I've got is the truth. We don't know who we are until we do.

We pull up to the diner parking lot. Tank knows the drill. I hand him a hundred-dollar bill, and he hops out and runs inside while I idle in the lot.

As I wait, I look through the rolled-down passenger window at the activity inside. There are waitresses and busboys. Families at tables and people sitting solo at the long counter. Tank props one ass cheek on a stool at the counter while an older woman with thick white hair gives him a warm grin.

He makes small talk with her, and she stuffs extra condiments and napkins into the bag. She looks happy and healthy, at least from this distance. It's as close as I ever allow myself to get to her.

I blink at the sight and look away as Tank heads back through the lot carrying a big plastic bag with the name Savage written in black marker. He sets the bag in the back, then climbs into the front.

"She said I have to stop overtipping her," Tank chuckles. "Threw in a year's supply of napkins and shit."

The scents of my food, Claire's, and Tank's turkey dinner fill the truck as I head back toward the compound. "As long as she took it."

That's all that matters.

After everything I did to her, it's the least I can do.

FOUR
CLAIRE

AURORA'S HAD her first decent meal in a while. I didn't have to water down the powder, and she loved every bit of it.

I have to imagine being in an air-conditioned room with a comfortable crib—not to mention a full belly—is going to give her one of the best nights of sleep of her life. I'm in the bathroom washing my hands and cleaning the baby food off the towel Aurora used as a bib when I hear a knock.

As I rush to open the door, I look at Aurora. She's still sound asleep, her little mouth open as she dreams. I take a breath and open the door just a crack to Savage. He's holding a large plastic bag in his arms, and he narrows his eyes as he looks past me.

"Oh shit," he whispers. "Did I wake her? I'm so sorry. I should have texted you to let you know I was headed back. I didn't think."

I stare at him for a second, not sure what's more

shocking. That he apologized. That he noticed Aurora was asleep. Or that he would bother to text me to let me know he was heading back. I don't know how to process any of this. I stare at him, unblinking.

"What should I do here?" he asks, looking so genuinely confused that I have to smile.

It's then that I notice how unbelievably handsome Savage is. His dark brown eyes are on the small side, but they show a warmth of light and sincerity as he stares at me. He has dark brown hair that curls slightly at the ends. He's not wearing his sunglasses so I can see his whole face, and it's a gorgeous face, the face of a man who has sharp edges but softness underneath. He has a square jaw, bristled from a day or two of not shaving. His nose is large, but in a good way. He looks like the hero in an action movie—not perfect in a forgettable, symmetrical way.

He swallows, and I see his Adam's apple move in his throat. "Claire," he says, his voice a thick whisper. "Should I leave your dinner? Do you want to have one of the girls stay with the baby so you can eat somewhere other than your room?"

I can't believe he's giving me a choice. I want so badly to say something. I want to invite him in, but it's like my brain and my body are in a war. I think about what Anthony would have said or done, and it's like I go on autopilot.

"Whatever you want, babe," I say, looking down at the floor.

I realize what I said as soon as the words leave my

mouth. My eyes fly to Savage's, and I duck my chin, not sure if he's going to scream or worse. To my continued surprise, he laughs.

"Babe?" He lifts a brow. "Better than asshole, I guess." He nods toward the baby. "You want to eat alone, or you want some company? I can join you or give you space. This is not my call, Claire. You're the boss in this room."

I swallow back a hurricane of emotions—fear, confusion, and, most of all, gratitude. "Come in?" I say quietly. "I think she's in a food coma."

Savage practically tiptoes into the room, and he sets the plastic bag on the coffee table so quietly that I almost laugh out loud.

"Savage," I tell him. "We lived with bikers. Way worse noises than what you all have here. She could probably sleep through a tornado."

He nods thoughtfully, like he's paying attention and actually learning a little something about babies. "That's a real useful skill to have in a compound full of loudmouth idiots." He smiles at me. "I can't promise I won't be one of them, but I will try to keep my voice down."

He starts setting up the food on the table, handing me the straw that goes along with my soda. "If that's watered down too much, I'll have Stella bring you another one. She's the one who went to the store for the diapers. She works for us, so you need anything—food, drinks—just let her know, and she'll add it to the list.

Don't feel bad asking. We pay her for her work around here."

I'm slowly starting to develop a picture of this club. The guys who live here, the women in their lives. I'm not sure how I ended up in this place and how I'll ever find my way to independence, but I'm relaxing just enough to feel more than fear, stress, and resentment.

Savage unpacks a smaller bag from within the big bag. "This," he tells me, "is a burger that you're going to dream about. And the sweet potato fries have salt flakes." He shakes his head as if this is a true culinary wonder. "Now, I know you asked for regular fries, but I got both. I hope you don't mind sharing, because I'm telling you…the salt flakes add something special, Claire."

He rolls his eyes back in his head and makes a kissing sound. I think my mouth falls open a little. I'm surprised, yeah, but not at this biker's enthusiasm for fries. I'm honestly shocked that he's so relaxed. He isn't angry about anything—not that I can tell. He just spent a shit-ton of money on food, and yet, an undercurrent of peace spreads in the room.

He lifts his chin toward the bag. "Dig in." He unwraps a round black plastic container, peels back the clear lid, and flicks a look at me. "Do I have to watch my language around the baby when she's asleep?"

I shake my head. "She can't talk yet. I don't think she knows the difference between fuck and frog. You have a few months, I think, before she starts copying what she hears." What I don't say is there is no way we'll still be here in a few months. By the time his language could be a problem, we'll be long gone. God, at least I hope we will, even if I have no idea how that's going to happen.

When he opens the container, the most delicious fragrance fills the room. It's like home-cooked heaven.

He unwraps some plastic cutlery and spears a piece of meat, a bunch of carrots, and a few potatoes soaked in gravy with a fork, and he puts it all on the lid of the carryout container like it's a spare plate. Then he extends the entire thing my way.

"You've got to try this," he says. "I'll trade you for some of those fries."

I take a long sip of the soda, and the carbonation makes my eyes water in the best way. I blot a tear from the corner of my good eye—the one that isn't swollen and bruised—and sigh. "Oh my God, Savage. That tastes good."

He quirks a brow at me. "That's sugar water, Claire. You think that's good, you have to try the food."

I take the fork and pick up a small bite of beef and a piece of carrot. I sniff it, close my eyes, and pop the entire thing into my mouth. "Holy crap," I mumble. "What is that?"

"Beef stew," he says. "Definitely not hot weather food, but I don't give a fuck. It's my favorite. It's fucking delicious." He looks at the coffee table as if he's just noticed something's missing. "I need a beer," he says, getting up.

I let myself look down his long legs in very dark

denim jeans as he stands. He's muscular, like never been an ounce overweight in his life muscular. He's shed his leather vest and put on a plain white T-shirt that looks immaculately clean and which reveals heavily tattooed arms.

He points at me as he pulls open the door. "You want anything? Cold beer? Fresh soda?"

I shake my head, and he turns to go, but then he cocks his head and looks back at me. "I told you this is your room," he says, a sly grin on his face, "but if you lock me out just so you can eat my stew…"

I laugh for real then, and a smile covers my face. "I'll slide a sweet potato fry under the door for you."

He gives me an exaggerated scowl and fake growls, then grins at me. "I can't say I'd blame you if you did."

He leaves me alone then, the door closing quietly behind him. I honestly can't understand this man. He just spent money to buy my freedom. He bought baby food and diapers. There was even a little T-shirt and a pair of pajamas in the bag for Aurora. Why?

He seems sweet and gentle, caring, even. All wrapped up in a bad-ass package.

I take another bite of the stew and even try some of my burger and fries while he's gone. It's all so delicious. And no one is angry, yelling, complaining. This is too easy. Too good. Whether I deserve it or not, for as long as it lasts, I'm going to hold on to it. Get strong and plan my escape. Because no matter how sweet and easy everyone is right now, I know it's only a matter of time, and nothing good lasts for very long.

I don't know if it's the soft bed or the cool room, the peace and quiet, or the lack of swearing and pounding outside my door, but I get the best night's sleep I've had in years.

It's not until Aurora starts cooing loudly that I open my eyes. I immediately remember where I am and how we got here.

Last night after we ate, Savage cleaned up all the mess we made, took my leftovers to the kitchen, and made me promise that I'd drink water and take the meds to help with the swelling.

The room is comfortable and silent.

No one is bothering us.

I can hardly believe this is real.

I mix up formula for Aurora after changing her diaper and putting her in the little T-shirt with the same pajama pants from last night. After she finishes her bottle, I take a fast shower, luxuriating in the hot water and sweet-smelling toiletries.

We're safe.

At least for now, and that's everything.

When I get out of the shower, the phone that Savage bought me is lit up with a message. I tighten the towel around myself and read it.

> Savage: Poppy's at work, so Stella's gonna take you shopping for clothes. She's got the money. Get what you need. I'll see you tonight.

I have two other messages.

> Unknown: Hi, Claire!! It's Poppy. I'm working today, but I wanted you to have my number. Check in if you need anything. I've got Phantom on the hunt for a baby bathtub for Aurora. If you need anything today, let the girls at the compound know, and they'll take care of you. Talk soon.

I'm trying to read the next text when there is a light knock at the door. "Claire, it's Stella. I have coffee."

I look down at the phone and see that Stella did text ten minutes ago that she was coming by with coffee.

"One second," I call out. I run into the bathroom, put back on the same clothes I wore yesterday, take my hair out of the towel and finger-comb it, and then I unlock the door and open it a crack.

The girl who went shopping with Savage is standing at the door with a huge grin and a travel mug in her hand. "Tell me you drink coffee," she says dramatically.

I nod.

"Cream? Sugar? Nothing? I'll run back to the kitchen for whatever you want."

I shake my head. "You didn't have to do that."

She waves a hand at me. "No bother, but this one is mine. I need to know how you take yours if you don't want to come out and make it yourself."

Just then, little Aurora stands up in her crib and grips the wooden bars with her chubby fingers.

"Holyyyy shit." Stella shakes her head. "I don't have

a maternal bone in my body, but that baby is gorgeous. Look at you." She lowers her face and wiggles her fingers at my daughter. "Those eyes. They are crystal blue." She looks at me and crosses her arms over her chest. She grimaces and then continues. "I want to kick the ass of whoever did that to your eye, but I'm going to leave the violence to the boys. Now, where'd your daughter get those blue eyes?"

"My mom," I say, and I can't stop the smile that comes. "My mom's were the exact same shade of blue."

Stella frowns and flips her hair over her bare shoulder. Her red tank top is bedazzled with glittery stones, and the color really shows off her dark tan. "Were? Ugh, I'm sorry. How long has your mom been gone?"

I choke back my answer when Stella holds up a hand. "Don't answer that. I'm prying in your business and making an ass of myself, when I'm here trying to make friends." She stands up to her full height. "I'll be back in five minutes with coffee, and if you don't tell me how you take it, I'm going to bring a little of everything. Are you a breakfast person? We've got fruit, bagels. Any basic shit you want, we probably have."

My head is spinning with how fast Stella is talking and all the options she's throwing my way.

Stella doesn't wait for an answer. She drops her coffee on my coffee table and sweeps toward the door.

She heads down the hallway, and I can hear the clacking of her high-heel shoes as she walks. Stella is pretty, in a very done-up way. Long nails, fancy pedicure, short shorts, but she seems as genuine as they come.

I'm still rooted to my spot, thinking about all the things happening around me and to me, when Stella arrives back, knocks lightly, and then lets herself in. I realize immediately that I didn't lock the door behind her.

Stella chatters on while I drink the coffee she brought and eat a banana—feeding some of it, along with baby oatmeal, to Aurora. Then I pack a few diapers in one of the plastic bags from yesterday.

"Oh shit." Stella frowns.

"What's wrong?" I ask, my stomach sinking. "Did I do something wrong?"

Stella cocks her head. "Baby, no. You're perfect. You don't have a purse, a diaper bag. Nothing. Do you have a wallet or ID?"

I nod. I had my ID in the back pocket of the shorts I wore yesterday. It's sitting on the bedside table beside the phone Savage got me.

"All right, then. You ready to go?" She points to the closet, where some shoes are lined up. "Those are mine, and I swear, baby, I do not have feet cooties. We'll get you a whole new wardrobe today."

I slide my feet into a pair of tennis shoes that are a little big, but they'll work. Then I pick up Aurora. "Honestly, it's fine. Thank you so much for doing all this."

We're about to head out when I suddenly stop. I reach for Stella's arm. Her skin is so soft, and she's so…

I don't know. Beautiful in her own way. She has an ease about her that I recognize. It's how I used to be. Young, free. Unbroken. I envy that for myself, but it brings me a lot of peace to see that a woman who's here all the time isn't miserable. Her easy manner gives me the guts to ask her the question that's been burning in my brain since yesterday.

"Yeah, babe?" she asks, turning to me.

"I don't understand," I tell her softly. "Why is he doing this? You, Poppy? Why are any of you doing all this for me?"

Stella blows out a big breath through glossy bright-red lips. "Right," she says. "Yeah, of course. I get what you're asking." Then she looks me in the eye. "Most people with great lives and stable families don't join our club," she says quietly. "Some do, I'm sure, but none that I know." She looks down at her nails and grimaces. "Every man out there, every woman who hangs around here... We all came from something bad or worse than bad. We're here because this is a place where other people who come from equally effed-up shit can get away from it all. Find something good in all the anger and the violence and the poverty."

She swallows and is quiet for a second.

"We're all strays in our own way. But just because we're a random pack of lost souls doesn't mean we don't make some kind of family together." She brightens a little. "You fit in here," she assures me. "Don't worry so much about it."

She stalks toward the door and suddenly turns to

face me. "Oh. I forgot. Savage picked up a car seat. You should have seen him trying to install it. It was like a bad joke—how many bad-ass bikers does it take to install a baby seat?"

She cackles and waves for me to follow her. I tuck my new phone into my pocket and leave my room. I only realize when I'm walking back through the compound that I forgot the key. I didn't lock my room.

I somehow trust that, locked or not, nothing bad will happen. And that feeling, for the first time, feels like freedom.

Stella leads me through the compound, and I duck my head, avoiding what feels like stares from a couple of women I don't know and a bunch of bikers. Some are shirtless, watching TV and drinking coffee. Others are wearing sunglasses and talking on their phones or to one another. The vibe here is so different. At the Hellfires' compound, you felt like a fight could break out at any moment. Power was traded and taken. The strong bullied the weak.

This place feels weirdly like a family. People shout "Morning!" to no one in particular. I clutch Aurora to my chest and follow Stella, who is shouting at people, making fun of others, and just generally acting like she's the big sister of everyone in this place.

As we head past the bar, Phantom, who I now know is the president of the club, stops Stella with a nod of his head.

"Hey, handsome," she drawls.

Phantom shakes his head. "Stel, come on. Poppy

hates when you call me that." But he's stifling a grin under a thick, dark beard.

"Liar, Poppy doesn't mind. She wears that shit like a badge of honor. You may be handsome, but that girl is way prettier than you could ever be. You really climbed that ladder."

Phantom holds up a hand. But one corner of his mouth lifts, and he looks at me. "Savage takin' good care of you?"

"I don't think I'll ever be able to thank him, thank you. You've all—" I choke a bit on the word "—saved us."

Phantom lowers his brows in a terrifying glare and waves a hand at me. "I wasn't looking for thanks. I just... Ah fuck." He pulls a wad of cash out of his back pocket and nods at Stella. "Savage set you up?"

Stella pats a black leather purse that's over her shoulder. "He sure did." She leans in and loudly whispers, "He gave me a grand, and I'm planning on spending every penny."

My mouth drops open. A thousand dollars? Savage gave Stella a thousand dollars to spend on me and the baby? I must have misunderstood.

Phantom gives her a bunch more cash. I don't look at it. I don't want to know how much he's giving her or what they plan to use it for. He talks in a low voice to Stella while I bounce Aurora in my arms.

"Yo, we goin'?" A huge guy I've never seen before comes out of the kitchen, brushing crumbs from the front of his black T-shirt.

"Claire, this is Tank. He'll be driving you today." Phantom claps the guy on the shoulder. "Take good care of them, you hear me?"

Tank widens his eyes at Aurora. "As long as I don't have to play baby music in the truck, I'm good. Ready to go?"

"We're ready," Stella tells him, thankfully saving me from speaking because I'm not sure I could without my voice wavering.

What kind of crazy fairy tale did I step into, and am I going to wake up in a different reality?

I sure as fuck hope not.

FIVE
SAVAGE

I SPEND the day doing the shit I least like doing, but which is a critical part of my role in the club. I have to update our security system.

The compound is massive as far as compounds go, and we have the place reinforced for all kinds of emergencies. We have storm protection systems in place, generators, and an entire garage full of vintage cars. We have cash, guns, and even some other substances that would excite federal law enforcement if they had a clue what goes on behind our closed doors.

A club like ours can only fly under the radar if we're careful, and my entire job is being careful. Careful to stay ten steps ahead of the law, our enemies, and our rivals. I'm no techie, but we have a few guys we trust and pay well for that trust, so after hours of thinking about upgrades and the cost, I meet with our guy off-site.

That's another layer of protection I put between the

club and the outside world. Our tech guy Ricardo thinks my name is Sam Sloane. Sam owns a boat repair business on the coast, and he's been screwed over before—by both the Coast Guard and the mafia. Ricardo isn't exactly friendly with guys with badges either, so we meet in public places, and we talk about logistics and what I need to buy.

Ricardo has never seen my fictional boatyard. He's never tested me on my knowledge about boats—of which I have none—and that's why he keeps me as a paying customer. After Ricardo and I finish our tacos at a hole-in-the-wall joint an hour outside of town, I load up brand-new, unboxed equipment in my truck.

As I'm leaving, a thought occurs to me. "You got any laptops, tablets, or shit like that?" I ask.

Ricardo nods. "What you thinking of running on it?"

I shake my head. "This is for personal use. Basic email and internet. I'm due for an upgrade."

He heads over to his truck and brings back a laptop, new in the box. "This doesn't have a ton of memory on it. You won't be able to game or anything that requires a lot of processing power, but email and basic online shit, this'll do you fine."

"Add it to my total," I tell him.

He waves a hand. "Consider it a gift."

I shake his hand and clap him on the back, then head back to the compound.

On the drive, my mind bounces around like a tennis ball. I think about Claire and how she's doing today.

Stella has sent me a couple of pictures and texts, updating me on the clothes and shit they are buying, but I don't care about what they buy. I care about how Claire's doing. Is she quiet and withdrawn? Is she starting to talk more? Share more? I ask a few questions, and Stella is quick to answer.

> Stella: No, not really. But she's smiling a lot, and that's something.

Stella sends me a selfie of herself with a giant, goofy grin and Tank looking incredibly bored as they wait outside a dressing room.

> Stella: She also won't let her baby out of her sight, which doesn't surprise me. Even trying on clothes and shoes, Claire takes Aurora in with her, as if she is worried someone is going to take her.

That also doesn't surprise me. I thumbs-up the post but don't say more. I head back to the compound and get to work setting up the equipment. Shadow is there to help, climbing ladders to pull down the old cameras and attaching new, state-of-the-art, wireless equipment, when a thought occurs to me.

"Could we set these up in Claire's room?" I ask.

Shadow gives me a glare so hot it could fry an egg. "You thinking about monitoring her room?" he asks. "That's fucked, man."

I shake my head. "Fuck no. My God. I'm thinking she can watch the baby on the security cams. That way, you know, she wants to come out and eat dinner or cook something, she can leave the baby sleeping or whatever."

Shadow rubs his jaw with two fingers and laughs. "You clearly didn't spend much time on Phantom and Poppy's baby registry."

I lift my hands at him as if to ask what the fuck that means. "No, I kicked cash into the kitty with everybody else."

Shadow laughs. "Violet and I spent hours on that damn site. Consider yourself lucky. I don't know if my old lady's getting baby fever again or what. Anyway, point being, there's such a thing as a baby monitor. You don't need high-tech surveillance to check on a sleeping kid."

I feel somewhat stupid for not knowing that, but how the hell would I? It's not like I know shit about babies or how to monitor them. But the more I think about Claire being here, the more I want to do to make sure she's safe. Comfortable. And that whatever she needs to spread her wings a little, leave her room if and when she wants to, she has it.

I nod at Shadow, and we head into Phantom's office to test the equipment. That's when I get a text.

> Tank: We're stopping for lunch at the diner. You want me to bring you something back? Also, that waitress got our table today, and she thinks I'm you. You want me to say something? So she doesn't think I'm Savage?

I reply back fast.

> Me: Nah, I'm good. And just let it go. She doesn't need to know anything. You got cash to tip her?

> Tank: Yup.

We go back to walking Phantom through setting up the new cameras. As soon as we're done, I check the registry for Poppy and Phantom on my phone. I didn't even bother reading it when Stella sent it a couple months ago, but now, I get in my truck and head to the store where they registered.

By the time I get back to the compound, it's almost dinnertime. I've got a couple more bags of shit in the back, but on a whim, I head back to the diner. It's not likely she'll still be there, but it's not far out of the way. I park my truck in the lot and squint into the glare of the setting sun through the plate-glass windows.

I see her then, her thick white hair moving as she nods at a couple. She's taking their order, and from this distance, that's really all I can see.

I'm doing this for you, I think. *For us.*

I throw the truck in drive and head back to the compound, not letting myself think or feel anything. That's how it has to be. That's how I can put the past behind me and focus on moving forward.

Right here and now.

Not then.

Not who I was.

Not who I couldn't be.

I head into the compound and find Stella sitting on Tank's lap, eating a plate of hot wings. I shake my head. She's a shameless flirt. Stella's probably fifteen years older than Tank, and the kid seems a lot more interested in playing video games than balancing Stella's long legs on his lap, but it's good to see they didn't kill each other after a day of shopping.

When Stella sees me, she points toward the hallway that leads to the bedrooms. "She's feeding the baby," she calls. "I told her to come eat wings with us, but she said she was full from lunch."

I nod and head down the hallway, a weird excitement in my gut. It's stupid, for sure, to think anything. To feel anything for this woman. She's a widow of sorts. A single mother. A woman who's got a long road ahead of her before she can even think about dealing with whatever she left behind, but I feel my fist tighten around the plastic bag I'm carrying. Why the hell are my hands sweating?

I lightly knock on the door. "Claire, it's—" But I don't have time to get the words out before the door opens, and my jaw nearly drops to my chest.

Claire is dressed in her new clothes. She's wearing a long yellow sundress and gold-colored flip-flops on her feet. Her hair is long and loose, and now that it's dry and down—not in a messy, matted bun—I can see it's a gorgeous chestnut-brown color. She's not wearing makeup, but her cheeks are flushed pink and there is the slightest hint of peach gloss on her lips. Her black eye is still swollen and angry-looking, but the rest of her is breathtakingly beautiful.

I stare at her, my mouth open, and I don't say a thing.

"Savage?" She looks at me, her lips parted. "Are you okay?"

I hear Aurora babbling behind her, and the sound of the baby breaks me out of my trance. "Baby," I blurt out, holding up the bag like I'm some kind of trick-or-treater expecting candy. "Here."

She widens her eyes a bit and looks down at the bag. "What did you do now?" She shakes her head, and the long, long hair swishes over her bare shoulders. "Savage…" She motions down at her dress. "Look at this."

"I am." The words slip out before I can stop them. "Claire, you're…stunning."

She looks shocked and takes a step back. "I'm not," she murmurs.

"Jesus, stop." I look her over and can't let this woman deny what she is. She's beautiful. How the fuck could anybody have this woman and treat her like anything but a goddess? I don't say it, though. Instead, I blurt out, "You're…incredible."

"Uh, thank you." She looks uncomfortable at the compliment and motions down at herself with a hand. "Some nice clothes and a shower, and not one, but two incredible meals at the diner apparently change a person. The clothes, the shoes… I don't know how to thank you for all of this, Savage."

She flicks a look at me, and something passes between us. Something that I never would have imagined when I first saw her sweating and cowering in Mad Dog's shit truck. My heart rate picks up, and sweat breaks out along my hairline. I shove aside every instinct that tells me to move closer to her.

She's in no position for me to make any moves—I can't even think about it. I promised her she'd be safe here, and I'm not going to do anything to threaten that. And what the fuck is wrong with me anyway? She's somebody's mama and some dead guy's widow. The last thing she's thinking about is me.

I shake my head and will any thoughts I have about Claire—her beautiful hair, her gorgeous skin—far from my mind. I shake the bag I'm holding like it's weighed down by feral cats. "For you," I tell her.

She takes the bag and motions for me to come in. Little Aurora is lying on a colorful rug, playing with new toys. When she sees me, she gurgles, which is about the only noises the kid can make.

Claire smiles, and the warmth and love that I see on her face is so immense, I honestly do feel like I've saved a life. Maybe two. And based on the way I feel with them—protective, intrigued—I know now for sure I did the right thing. I can't believe that the same woman who would hardly whisper, could hardly get out of the truck yesterday, is now beside me looking over her daughter with such pride.

"She can't crawl yet, but I blame myself for that," Claire explains, kicking off her flip-flops and lowering herself to sit on the floor beside her daughter. She crosses her legs under her, takes a bright pink and purple toy train, and pushes it along the road that is inked into the play mat. "I've carried her just about everywhere her entire life. I discouraged her from exploring and crawling. There wasn't a lot in our room with the Hellfires that was kid-friendly."

I can't believe she's opening up to me, and I debate what to do. Kick off my boots and sit down with her? Sit on the bed? The couch? It all feels so personal. Like I'm in her space, even though she's our guest. I settle for sitting back on the couch and watching from a safe distance.

"She's smart," I say, because I believe it with my whole heart. "She'll catch up."

Claire nods. "I think it's the food too. Her coloring looks better to me. Babies are so resilient."

She goes quiet then, and I have to fight my entire body. I want to go to her. To reassure her that adults are resilient too. That I'm sorry she and her daughter have to be strong like they are. That they can now breathe and just heal. They deserve it after all they've been through.

As much as I want to comfort Claire, I'm not sure what I believe. If I believe that we can fully get over the shit that kicked us down and beat us bloody in our pasts. But if there is anyone on this earth I want that healing for, it's Claire.

She peeks at the bag I brought. "What are these?" she asks.

I clear my throat against the clot of emotion that feels lodged in my sternum. "A baby monitor," I tell her. "So, you can keep an eye on your girl if you want to cook in the kitchen or even just leave the room to hang out with the assholes." I chuckle. "Or Stella. She'll introduce you to the other girls, but getting any of them to play babysitter..." I shake my head. "If you're comfortable, use it."

Claire's eyes—even the bruised one—widen when she pulls the slim box holding the brand-new laptop from the bag. "Savage... I can't..."

"You can," I tell her. "You got family, use the phone. I'll re-up the plan if you use all the minutes. You want to email anybody, read the news, I don't know..." I gesture toward the device. "It's a low-end model, but I figured something's better than nothing."

I motion for her to hand me the box, and I peel the plastic wrapper off it. "I run the security system here, so I can help you get it set up, get on the Wi-Fi. You can create all your passwords for privacy, but I can fire this up if you'd like."

She nods and holds Aurora's toy between her fingers while she stares off into the distance. "I'd like to start looking for jobs," she says quietly. "I haven't worked in a while, though. I don't know what I'd do for day care. I'm not ready to leave Aurora, but I'd like to find a way to pay you back."

I shake my head. "Fuck that," I say. "Sorry, Aurora. You want a job because you want a job, you go for it. There's no debt here, Claire. I'm not keeping a tally."

"But I am," she says. She bites her lower lip and looks at me. "I used to be someone, Savage. A whole person. I had a family and a career. I have an education and hobbies." A silent tear streaks down her cheek, and it takes everything I have in me not to lean forward, drop to my knees, and wipe it away. "You're not seeing the whole story. Just a really, really shitty chapter."

Anger and sadness start a bare-knuckle fight in my chest. "I know that," I croak out. "You don't have to explain it. I know."

She lifts her face to me, an unasked question so clear on her face it's like I can read her mind. How do I know?

"I've had more than one shitty chapter," I tell her as I turn on the laptop and punch in the Wi-Fi, then hand the device back to her. "The only reason I want to do so much for you is because this club, this place, did so much for me when I was at my most fucked up."

I'm starting to wonder if that's not the only reason I want to help Claire. But again, I can't think those thoughts. "She's all yours," I tell her.

Claire stands cautiously and sits beside me on the couch. "I used to work at a law firm, but I haven't used a computer in almost two years."

I turn to look at her. What the hell has she been

through that she hasn't had a computer or access to one in two years?

I don't ask because I do not want to know. I just thank my lucky stars that Anthony is already dead. If he were still around, I don't know that helping Claire would be enough to satisfy me.

If my history is any indication, I won't see justice served until the abuser is made to pay. But he's out of the picture, and I'm going to have to channel my anger someplace else.

Claire is leaning close to me, looking at the laptop screen, when we both hear Aurora say very, very quietly, "Ma-ma."

Claire leaps off the couch, a stunned and deliriously happy look on her face. She swoops down, picks up her baby, and lifts her high in the air. "Did you just say that? Did my big girl just say Mama? Aurora." She taps the bright sunshine on the new T-shirt that covers her daughter's chest and then taps her own chest. "Mama. Aurora said Mama."

Aurora blows a spittle-covered raspberry and giggles quietly. Claire turns to me. "You heard her, didn't you? Tell me you heard her say Mama."

"She sure did," I say, grinning. "Was that her first time?"

"The first time she did it so clearly. You said Mama." Claire is beaming at her daughter, then looking back at me, radiant with joy, sharing this event with me.

I want to celebrate this moment with them. To savor every second of happiness, love, and progress that these milestones represent. But I can't. This hurts too much. I can't watch her be a good mother, to love on her daughter, despite all they have been through together. I start to wonder where Claire and Aurora would be now if Anthony hadn't died. If Mad Dog hadn't been willing to sell them like used car parts.

I'm not angry that she didn't leave sooner. I know why she couldn't. Why she didn't. At least, I'm damned sure I think I understand. I've spent years processing why women like Claire get trapped. How they get stuck in a situation that starts as love and ends in violence. How they keep their babies in horrible circumstances while taking the worst of it with their faces, their hearts, and their souls.

I'm just not able to deal with the fact that this goodness, freedom, and hope… That's what's ahead for Claire and Aurora. They deserve it, that's for fucking sure. But not everybody gets that. I want it for her, for them, I do. But goddamn, I want it for me. I want it for the kid who got the black eyes. Who hid his face, his voice, his needs—until he couldn't.

My mama was proud of me once…just once. And then I threw it all in a dumpster, doused it with gas, and tossed a match right on top. I did it because it was the right thing to do, but goddamn if it doesn't still hurt.

I thought I got through all this years ago, buried the past once and for all and moved the fuck on. But clearly, being around Claire and Aurora has me dredging up shit I thought I had buried.

It all hurts more than I can take. Watching Claire

right now is like a beautiful dagger through my heart. I'm not over what happened to me. What I lost. What I gave up.

I can't be here, can't see this.

I've got to fucking go.

I leap up from the couch. "Right. You're all good here, so I'm going to go. Stella will take care of your dinner tonight," I tell her. Then I yank open the door and get my ass out of that room as fast as my boots will take me.

SIX
CLAIRE

SAVAGE LEAVES in a bit of a rush, but I'm too excited about Aurora saying Mama to think too much about it. Maybe he has work to do or something came up. I'm glad he was here to share this happy event with me, though. As strange as it sounds, I like his company, and it may not be smart of me, but I'm getting used to the way he treats me.

I'm getting used to how everyone acts around here.

I'm getting used to not always being afraid.

I wonder if Aurora's new word would have happened without the great food, peaceful rest, and the kindness everyone here has shown us.

I owe all of this to Savage.

After he leaves, I play with Aurora and feed her dinner, then give her a bath as best I can in the bathroom sink and change her for bed. Even if she doesn't understand that she's reached a new milestone, I think all my excitement has made her a little fussy. I struggle to settle her down and get her to sleep. She keeps sitting up in the crib and calling, "Mama. Mama." Now that she knows how that works, I have a feeling I'm going to be hearing a lot of it.

Once she's dozing off in the crib, I set up the baby monitor. I don't plan on using it, but I don't want it to go to waste. Maybe I can shower at night after she goes to sleep and bring the monitor into the bathroom with me.

I settle onto the couch with the laptop Savage gave me. I can hardly believe I have one, and even if I don't keep it forever, I can use this to look for a job and write up a new résumé. The possibilities have me nearly giddy.

I do wish Savage had stayed to hang out with me, though. It's a weird thing to feel, and an even weirder thing to admit, but he has a gentle confidence.

It's like he thinks problems are just things to be solved and not earth-shattering tragedies. Everything that happened made Anthony angry, and while I loved him once, by the time I got pregnant with Aurora, I was so exhausted managing his reactions to things, I shifted to trying to prevent problems just so I wouldn't have to deal with his rage later.

But that's the thing about life.

You can never stop it from happening.

I open a browser on the laptop and search for any information I can find about Anthony's accident. There isn't much. Just a small write-up in the local news. Not even his name is included. If I didn't know the details already, I'd never know for sure that this was about him.

Local Man Dies in Motorcycle Accident

Officers responded to a call of a motorcycle overturned on SR 19. Damage to the bike appeared consistent with a side impact. No other vehicles or witnesses to the incident were on the scene. The rider, a male in his early thirties whose identity is being withheld pending notification of his next of kin, was found deceased several feet away. Injuries appeared consistent with being thrown from the motorcycle, but the investigation is ongoing.

It's hard to summon any emotions reading the article. Yes, I know this is my daughter's father they are writing about. Yes, he's dead, and he's never coming back. I cried my eyes out for two days over losing the financial security Anthony provided and for the man I once loved, but that part of him died a long time ago.

By the time I stopped crying, I realized how much worse things were going to get for me. Mad Dog and I fought constantly.

I wanted the club to give me Anthony's savings and let me and Aurora leave. But Mad Dog brought out a laundry list of shit Anthony had done, money he owed the club. The short answer was that I wasn't going to get anything, and I was going to be quiet and thankful they hadn't kicked me out on my ass the minute Anthony was gone.

Three days.

He'd only been gone three days when Savage found

me. The black eye I have now is the last thing Anthony ever gave me.

That was his choice.

His legacy was violence and cruelty.

It will not be what defines the rest of my life. Only that chapter.

And with the help of Savage and the people under this roof, I plan on rewriting my future.

I walk over to the crib and check on Aurora. She's sleeping peacefully, so I settle back on the couch and open another browser window. It's been years since I had access to a computer that wasn't ancient, and Anthony crushed my phone in our last fight so I've been cut off from everything for nearly a week.

I don't have the passwords to any of my old social media accounts memorized. Instead, I just Google one name: Dawn Taylor.

Immediately, a ton of old pictures and photos come up. Grainy clips posted to YouTube, gorgeous black-and-white images scanned to the internet from decades-old scrapbooks and photo albums from years ago. I load up a video on YouTube, turn the sound very low, and maximize the screen.

In the video, the band Neon Dawn takes the stage at a packed bar. The house lights are down, and a spotlight comes up on the lead singer, my mother, Dawn Taylor. She shakes the long waves of her chestnut-brown hair, eyes crystal blue like Aurora's underneath closed lids that sparkle with bright-blue eye shadow.

As the opening beats pick up, Mom opens her eyes, gives the crowd a sultry grin, and she sings. I watch video after video of Mom, aging through the years as Neon Dawn played small venues all over the country. When I finally reach the videos when Mom is pregnant with me, leaning on a stool as she sings, even with a massive belly, the tears start to come.

I miss her so much.

I wish she were alive now.

If she were, I might never have dated Anthony. Which means I'd never have Aurora. This is a drain I circle too many times in my head.

Anthony came into my life like a grief-busting tank, sweeping me onto his bike and into his life when I was so lost and so alone that all I wanted was a break from the sadness. I had no idea how to judge good from evil back then.

I am still all alone, but I don't feel that way. I could open the door to my room or send a text, and I believe in my heart that within five minutes, someone—Stella, Poppy, even Phantom—would be at my door with their arms, wallets, and hearts wide open.

And then of course, there is Savage. Who did all of that and more for me. Whether or not I'm naïve, I believe that he would do anything I asked and that we're truly safe. That no harm will come to me while I'm here under his protection and under the roof of the Hurricane Heat.

I hardly see Savage over the next week, but the time passes quickly. Stella visits me every morning, and Poppy stops by a couple times to chat. Shadow's wife Violet comes by and brings me an e-reader she's not using, and she sets me up with a digital library card, which is amazing.

Day by day, my eye heals, and my heart begins to think about what comes next. I miss seeing Savage and start to feel the urge to get out of my room. Aurora and I haven't been outside since the day we shopped, and other than showering and eating in the compound kitchen, I am already feeling a little anxious to get out in the world again.

I don't know where I'd go, though, or what I'd do.

Then I get an idea.

I grab my phone and send Savage a text.

> Me: Sorry to bother you, but do you think maybe Tank or someone could give me a ride today? I was thinking about going someplace to do some work on my laptop.

His reply comes back in minutes.

> Savage: Never a bother. How soon will you be ready?

I'm ready now. I already packed up Aurora's new diaper bag and slipped my laptop inside, so I tell him we're good and we can go anytime.

> Me: Anytime. Whenever it's convenient.

> Savage: I'll come get you.

A few minutes later, there's a knock at my door. I nearly launch myself toward it with a stupid grin on my face. "Hi," I say, holding the door open with a foot while I grab the diaper bag.

Today, I'm wearing my long hair loose. A black one-piece jumper may not be the most practical outfit, but after wearing those cutoff shorts for so many days, I don't even want to think about putting on shorts again. The top of the jumpsuit has tank-top-style straps that look like they are tied with bows, but which are sturdy enough that Aurora can grab on to my shoulders and not yank them down.

Savage's nostrils flare as he looks at my outfit from shoulders to toes. Then he locks his eyes on mine. He opens his mouth to speak but then says nothing. Just clamps his jaws together.

My stomach sinks. I feel like I've made him mad, and my confidence starts to waver.

"I'm sorry," I say. "Did I—"

He holds up a hand. "Don't apologize. You look fucking beautiful. Your eye is healing well. Your hair…" He shakes his head and runs a hand through his own hair. "I'm sorry. I've been staying away to give you space, and I'm sorry. I think I needed space too."

I try to gather up the pieces of my confidence.

Whatever is going on with him has nothing to do with me or anything I've done wrong.

"Are you okay?" I ask. "If you needed space, is it because I did something to upset you or stress you out?"

I prepare myself for whatever the answer is. I don't want this guy I hardly know to be mad at me. He's done so many things for us that maybe the money he's spent and the fact that Aurora will need new diapers soon is all getting to be too much.

Before he can answer, I move Aurora to my other arm and meet his eyes. "I'm going to start looking for a job," I tell him. "Aurora will need more diapers and baby food soon. I plan to get on my feet so I'm not your problem anymore. I want you to know that."

His eyes shift, and he looks at me with something that feels raw and vulnerable. I brace myself for what's coming. He's going to ask us to leave, or…

"You're not my problem," he growls, his words coming from a place deep in his throat. "Never fucking think that way."

A hot flush creeps its way along my chest. I feel my face go bright red. "Oh, um…" I don't know what to say. I'm not sure what he means. I've been nothing but trouble, at least financially, for him since the day he saved me. How could I not think that way when these people have done nothing but give and I've done nothing but take?

"Hey, boss." A voice from behind us breaks the

moment. Tank nods at me and waves at Aurora. "Hey there, sweetheart."

Savage startles and gives Tank a murderous look, but Tank throws up his hands in a surrender motion. "I was talking to the baby?" His eyes are wide, and he says it like a question. I mean, of course he was calling the baby sweetheart. Did Savage think Tank was talking to me? Was Savage jealous?

Savage's shoulders visibly relax, and he barks, "What is it?"

Tank jerks a thumb over his shoulder. "Phantom said there's a little problem that needs attention. He wants you in his office."

Savage blows out a breath. "Fuck. Okay." He turns to me and hands me a white envelope. "Spend what you need. This is for you." Then he turns to Tank. "Drive her wherever she wants to go. Stay close enough that you can get back to her fast when she tells you she's done. She's got work to do."

Tank looks totally unbothered that he's basically a chauffeur for me and Aurora for the day. He nods. "You got it, boss."

Savage looks at me like he's going to say something. He opens his mouth, and his eyes move from mine to my toes and then back. It's fast, not like a creepy look. His eyes dart everywhere as if he doesn't know where to look. But then he looks past me at Aurora and nods. "Later."

He says it like that's a complete sentence, and then he turns and heads back down the hallway.

Something flutters in my chest as I watch him walk in the opposite direction. I wish I knew why he was doing so much for me and my daughter. And I wish that I could turn off the very real way I'm starting to feel for him.

"Hey there, sunshine!"

I almost forgot that Tank was waiting. He ducks his head and is waving at Aurora, who lifts a chubby hand and waves back before sticking her fingers in her mouth.

I turn to the biker and give him a shrug. "Looks like you're stuck with me again."

"Claire," he says, giving me a look. "You know this is the cushiest gig we got goin' now, right?" He cocks his head. "Ten other assholes out there would kill to be the one to drive you around. I practically had to bust in some teeth so no one else volunteered."

He holds up his beefy hand in front of Aurora. "I've got a bet with the other guys that I can teach her how to high-five me. And I'm not going to win if I don't get some face time, you know what I mean?" He gives me a seriously pleading look. "She doesn't know how to high-five yet, does she?"

I laugh. "Uh, no." I set my diaper bag down on the floor outside my room, take Aurora's hand, and clap it to Tank's. "High-five," I say.

Aurora's eyes go wide at the clapping sound, and she bubbles spit over her little lips and says, "Ma ma ma."

Tank drops his hand like she burned him, and he

turns to me faster than I think a guy his size should move. "She's talking? Is that, like, her first word? Holy shit, I'm going to teach her to say Tank."

I shake my head and grab my bag. "One thing at a time," I tell him. "Let's focus on the high fives."

I don't really know anyplace else around here for us to go, and I'd really love a cold soda and some hot fries, so I have Tank drive us to the diner. The ride is short, and Tank tries to teach Aurora to say his name the entire way. She doesn't seem like she's in the mood to learn anything new this morning, but I let him chatter on as he drives.

"You want to come in?" I ask Tank. "You can eat something. Savage gave me money."

He shakes his head. "I had a lunch date today, and I was fucking nervous. I ate a whole large pizza minus one slice by myself. I'm stuffed."

"A date?" I unbuckle the car seat from the base so I can carry Aurora into the restaurant and have her sit beside me in a booth. "Tank, who's the lucky girl?"

His smile disappears as he turns in the driver's seat. "I'm the lucky one. She's somebody I know from high school. It's nothing. I mean, it was just lunch. I don't think she's that into me."

"She'd be a fool not to like you," I tell him. I hardly know the guy, but he has such a sweet, gentle soul. "Imagine what she's going to think when you teach a six-month-old how to high-five."

That gets him to laugh. "Practice time, kid. Hand

up." He holds up his hand, palm out, and I take my hand and high-five Tank.

I motion for Aurora to do it. She kind of smacks her hand in his direction, but it's enough to have him laughing.

"Yes. High-five, Aurora," he says.

"Ma ma mamama," she says, excited, even if she's not sure why.

I climb out of the back seat with my diaper bag and the car seat. Tank follows me into the restaurant and holds the door open while I walk in.

"You need me to do anything while you're workin'?" Tank asks.

"I could use another package of diapers. Do you mind?" I tell him the size Aurora needs and reassure him that he can't screw it up. "If you're worried, text me a picture before you buy them."

We agree that he'll come back to get me in two hours unless I text him to come sooner. He heads off to wash his truck and pick up my diapers, and I walk up to the hostess stand alone.

"Table for one?" A young girl, probably still in high school, grabs a menu and gives me a huge smile. "Or would you prefer a booth?"

"A booth would be great."

The girl brings us to a fairly quiet part of the diner, and as soon as I have Aurora settled with some toys, I try to look over the menu, but it's overwhelming with the number of options.

"Hi there, sweetie." A waitress wearing an orange

smock over a white golf shirt and tan pants greets me. "Well, my goodness. I don't think I've ever seen prettier eyes than these." She bends slightly to look at Aurora. "Hi there, angel."

I set down the menu. "Aurora, can you say hi?" I ask.

She smacks her hands together and says, "Maaaaa-ma maaaa-ma."

"We just learned that word," I tell the waitress, whose name tag reads Val.

"Well, that is the most important word of them all, isn't it?" Val turns to me and grins. She smooths down thick white hair that's cut to just below her chin and pulls out a little notebook. "Are we having food, sweetheart? Anything to drink?"

I didn't really bother looking, so I ask Val for some recommendations. I end up getting my favorite—the burger with sweet potato fries and a soda.

Val takes my order, and while Aurora busies herself with a toy, I get to work. It turns out to be a lot harder to get anything done in a restaurant with a six-month-old than I imagined.

When Tank comes back two hours later, I have little to show for the time out of my room. I was able to look up my old law firm, the one I worked at before, and I looked up some résumé samples online.

Val quickly comes back to greet Tank.

"Well, hello there, Savage," she says. "Is this your family?"

I look from Tank to Val. "This isn't Savage," I say,

but Tank and I are talking over each other, and I don't know if she hears me.

"Nah," Tank says. "These are just some friends. I'm the designated driver. That baby formula is powerful stuff. I can't let her get behind the wheel after a bottle or two."

Val laughs so hard and so sincerely, I think it actually heals me a little bit. I laugh, too, while Tank assures Val he doesn't need anything, and he'll see her next time.

She brings the check and I pay it, but I notice that Tank pulls out his wallet and adds some cash to the pile I leave on the table while I'm wiping Aurora's hands clean with a napkin.

"I left enough," I say quietly. "Savage gave me money."

He nods but then shrugs. "She's our regular waitress. Savage always tips her extra, so I figured he'd want me to."

Of course he does. Savage is a generous tipper. Probably nice to old ladies. Rescuer of women and children. But he's also a biker, maybe a criminal, and most definitely a mystery.

I shut down my curiosity and gather up my daughter and bag. I have no business thinking about him, let alone feeling anything for him. Not affection and sure as heck not curiosity either.

Tank grabs the car seat with Aurora in it while I pick up the diaper bag. And all of a sudden, for a moment, everything around me goes white. Panic settles in. I reach for Tank's arm, but then I stop myself and duck my head, bracing for a blow.

I almost grab my daughter back from him. But I can't. He'll get angry. He'll stop me. He'll take her away.

I clutch the top of the booth, snagging my palm in a smear of sticky syrup. I can't stop the racing thoughts, the instinctive panic that has me at war with myself.

He's not taking her.

He's not leaving with her.

He's only trying to help.

He's not Anthony.

I reassure myself with deep breaths, my nails digging into the side of the booth, until my heart rate calms. Tank takes about ten steps and looks back to where I'm still standing at the booth.

"You good?" he asks, lowering his brows and cocking his head. "You look pale."

Val, the waitress, comes up to us and starts clearing the table. She notes the large tip in cash and clucks her tongue. "Y'all shouldn't do that. You're too generous."

Tank suddenly looks uncomfortable. "Claire, you ready?"

No one seems aware of my freak-out. I look at Val and her warm, dimpled smile and Tank's look of mild confusion.

I'm the weirdo here. I'm the one who's broken. I'm the one who needs to listen when spoken to and go with the flow.

"Yeah," I whisper. "I'm ready."

Tank nods and waits, letting me walk ahead of him through the diner doors. When we get there, I stop and turn around. He's lightly swinging the car seat while talking to Aurora the whole time.

"Uncle Tank," he says. "I know it's a mouthful, but it's going to be your second word. I guess second and third words, but I've got faith in you, kid. Say it with me, Aurora. Uncle Tank."

She says, "Maaamaaamaa," but she answers him back.

Aurora looks at me as she says it, and something inside me crumbles. I feel tears sting my eyes, and I say, "Hey, baby."

"Uncle Tank." Tank's voice is so playful and happy as he tries to urge my daughter to say his name, I can't help but feel more assured and at ease.

And even though everything inside me feels panic and worry about letting this stranger carry my daughter, about how he's going to feel if I react or speak up, I fight the feelings. Because none of these people have done anything to even remotely suggest they might hurt me or my daughter.

We're safe.

SEVEN
SAVAGE

THAT DIDN'T FUCKING GO AS PLANNED.

When I get back to the compound, I have to be helped inside by Shadow and Viper.

"I'm fucking fine," I grunt, trying to shove myself upright, but I can't. I took a beating today, and while I won the fight, my body feels like it lost a title match.

I shrug off their help, trying to hide the pain that slices through my chest every time I move. I took a couple of boot kicks to the ribs and would not be surprised if I have bruises. I'll be lucky if nothing is fractured.

"You might have a concussion." Shadow grunts into my ear. "Lemme get you to your room, and we'll call the doc."

In addition to a lawyer, the club recently added a doctor to the payroll.

"Stop." I cover my face with my hands and let out a groan. I clearly didn't realize how many punches I took to the jaw, too. "I'm fine." I stand on my own, trying my ever-loving best not to pass out. "I'm going to check on Claire and the baby, and then I'll crash. If I need the doctor, you can call her in the morning."

I don't know why I'm hell-bent on checking on Claire after hardly seeing her at all for the last week. Part of me just wants to reassure myself that she's really here and okay. That she didn't pack up her laptop and her daughter and leave.

I lean one fist against her door and suck in a breath as I lift my hand to knock. Shadow and Viper are on my heels, glowering, hovering.

She opens the door, holding Aurora in her arms. "Savage?" She immediately looks worried. "What's wrong?"

I hold up a hand before Shadow or Viper can say anything. "How are you? Everything go okay today?" I try to sound normal, but my breath seems to be coming out real fucking shaky. A wave of nausea hits me, and my knees buckle.

"Oh my God." Claire turns and sets Aurora down in the crib, then she turns back. "Come in and sit down."

"He might need a doctor," Shadow says, and it sounds like he's gritting his teeth.

"I need a fucking babysitter like I need a hole in the head," I growl, glaring at him. I flick a look at Claire. "You mind? Can I sit a few?"

She nods, shoves a baby blanket and some toys off the couch, and motions for me to sit.

I drop onto the cushion, but as soon as I lower my body, an agonized noise slips past my throat.

Claire is immediately at my side. She kneels and hovers a hand over my arm. "What happened? Where are you hurt?"

Viper answers for me. "He took a few hits on a job today. Ribs, mostly. We want him to see a doctor, but—"

"I'm fucking fine." The words come out louder than I intend, and my first reaction is to look at Aurora in case I scared her. She's sitting up inside her crib, her wide crystal-blue eyes looking right into mine. "Sorry, baby," I mutter.

I lean back against the couch cushions and groan. "Lemme rest for five minutes, all right? If I don't catch my breath, we'll call in the doc."

Claire jumps to her feet and talks in a low voice with Shadow and Viper. They are chatting through something, but the second I close my eyes, I feel the first bit of relief from pain in hours.

The next thing I know, the door is closing, and Claire, Aurora, and I are alone.

"I'm fine," I try to tell her, "I just—"

I feel her hand on my arm, and the words die in my throat.

"I know you're not okay," she says, her voice calm but firm. "I'm going to take care of you, if you'll let me."

I open my eyes, and I don't know what's on my face, but she reaches forward and strokes my hair back from my face. "You don't need to worry about me," I tell her, but the words end on a cough. "I've been through worse."

"That doesn't mean you have to go through this alone now." She shakes her head. "I asked Shadow to bring some ice and ibuprofen. When was the last time you ate?"

She peppers me with questions while she lowers herself to the floor and helps me work my feet out of my boots.

"Glad I wore my cute socks today," I croak out. They're plain black, but at least they don't have holes or anything like that.

She gives me a wry smile and sets my boots by the door. Then she grabs all the pillows from the bed and lines them up on one of the armrests of the couch. "Do you want to move to the bed?" she asks. "Will that be more comfortable?"

"Unless you put me in a coffin, I don't want to move," I admit. My ribs burn like they are on fire. My jaw feels stiff and swollen at the same time. It hurts to talk, to hold my eyes open, to do anything. "Can I just lie here a few?"

"Of course." She helps me stretch my legs onto the couch, and I lie back. God help this woman, because I don't know if I'm going to be able to move again.

She puts a warm hand on my forehead, and I close my eyes. "I came to check on you," I grit out. "How was your day?"

She laughs softly as the couch dips. She's so close, her thigh touches my hip. I try to move to make more room for her, but trying to shift my torso makes me feel like someone is sawing into my rib cage with a very dull hacksaw.

I huff a hard breath, and she gasps.

"Shit. Sorry." She smooths my hair back, and there's a knock at the door. "Come in," she calls.

I hear voices and feel movement, but I start to let myself settle into the pain. Someone cups the back of my neck and holds my head up so I can swallow some chalky pills. Then my head is back against the pillows, and I feel a cool weight on my ribs. As soon as my head hits the pillow, I focus on the soft sound of Claire's voice, and I crash hard into sleep.

When I wake up, the room is mostly dark, except for one dim lamp. I can hear soft white noise, and I squint my eyes open.

"Hey, you're awake." Claire jumps off the bed where she was sitting with her laptop. She's changed into gray pajama pants and a matching button-down pajama top. Her hair is loose and free, and she looks tired.

"Sorry," I grunt. "I must have dozed off."

She nods and rests a hand against my forehead like I have a fever, but I ain't complaining. "How are you feeling? You can't have any more pain meds for about another hour."

"How long was I asleep?"

"It's five in the morning," she says with a smile.

There are soft shadows under her eyes, but she's looking at me sweetly.

"Holy shit, you've got to get some sleep. I'll get my ass up." I turn my head and realize the crib is gone. "Where's Aurora?" I demand, my pulse picking up. "Is she okay?"

Claire nods. "I moved the crib into the bathroom."

I'm confused. I lift a hand to my ribs and feel ice zipped into plastic bags and wrapped in towels under my T-shirt. It all starts to come together for me. "You've been taking care of me all night?" I ask.

"Just a few ice changes, and I rubbed a little of that pain gel you gave me on your jaw." She sweeps her fingertips lightly over my stubble. "You're probably going to have some bruises."

I swallow against the dryness in my throat. "Aurora," I croak out. "Why is she in the bathroom?"

Claire chuckles and sits so close beside me I can feel the soft curve of her thigh against mine. "I went to the kitchen to get ice a couple of times. I didn't want her to wake up, so I set up the baby monitor you got us and moved the crib into the bathroom. It's a bit snug if you need to use the bathroom, but she hasn't seemed to mind."

A few minutes of consciousness is all I have in me. I lift my hand to touch her. My head throbs. My face feels hot. But halfway to her cheek, I let my hand drop, close my eyes, and pass out again.

When I finally wake up again, I have to piss like crazy, and my head is throbbing. I squint open an eye and see an empty crib and unfamiliar surroundings. Then I see the play mat on the floor and remember—I'm in Claire's room.

"Claire?" I whisper, my voice scraping out of my parched throat like razor blades over a two-day growth of beard.

No one replies, so I hoist myself up on the couch. It takes a minute, but I am able to get up and off the couch, my left side screaming with soreness but nothing I haven't dealt with before. I consider heading back to my room, but my bladder doesn't have the patience that's going to require. I stumble into Claire's bathroom, close the door, and pee until I'm empty.

I wash my hands and face, groaning at the bruises that have popped up on my jaw. I open the door and see Claire's green eyes wide with worry.

"Savage," she breathes. "You're up. I left you alone for five minutes…"

"I'm a big boy," I tell her, but I need to steady myself against the doorframe. "I'll get out of your hair now. What time is it?"

Now that I've peed, I'm hungry, thirsty, and stiff as fuck from lying on the couch. I have shit to do today, and I'd better get to it.

"It's three," Claire says.

"Three?" I echo. "In the afternoon? I slept for almost twenty-four hours?"

She nods.

"Holy shit, I'm sorry. I'll get out of your space."

"No." Her voice is firm. The next thing I know, she's grabbing my hand in hers. "You're really hurt, Savage. Come on. I want you to lie down in my bed. I'll sleep on the couch. You shouldn't be alone until you're better."

I shake my head, but I leave my hand in hers. Her touch is strong, but her skin is so, so soft. "I'm all right," I tell her. "I'll take a few more pain relievers and sleep this shit off."

"No," she insists. "Listen to me. Phantom's daughters are here. They came after school. Aurora is having the time of her life out in the front, playing. I want to help you."

"I need to shower and eat. I probably smell like a three-day-old sock." I lick my lips. "Toothbrush. I've got to go take care of—"

Claire shakes her head. "You can shower here." Still holding on to my hand, she grabs her phone from her back pocket. "Text someone to go to your room and pack a bag of your stuff. You can stay here until you feel strong enough to stay alone. And you should probably see the doctor today." Her lips form a small frown. "I'm so worried you have a fractured rib, Savage. Please."

I am holding her hand and thinking, but the thoughts are coming too slowly. She trusted her baby with strangers. Holly and Daisy, Phantom and Poppy's daughters, are amazing and sweet, smart and kind. The fact that she trusted her baby to the girls means something more than I'm able to process right now.

"Shower," I say. "I feel disgusting. I need to freshen up."

She leaves me and grabs my cell phone from the coffee table. "Text someone," she says. "Or I'm going to go knocking on doors all the way down this hallway until I find your room."

One side of my mouth lifts in a smile, and I swear I'd have a full-face grin if my damned jaw didn't hurt so much.

Maybe this is just her way of paying me back. Maybe this is her caring. Either way, I'm not going to fight it.

"Hand me my phone," I say, and when I take it from her, I add, "Thank you."

I call Tank and tell him what to get from my room—towels, toiletries, and clothes. All the pillows from my bed, because even though she's been sleeping in her bed, I can tell Claire's been using a rolled-up towel because I had all the pillows on the couch.

Tank drops everything off in about five minutes, while Claire helps me peel off my socks. Once I kick Tank out, Claire puts my toiletries in her shower and my towels on the bar. She starts up the water while I brush my teeth, and then I go to take off my shirt, but goddamn, that hurts, and I stop moving entirely.

"Let me help." Claire gently grabs the hem of my T-shirt and lifts it over my middle. As the fabric moves past my ribs, she sucks in a loud breath. "Savage…" She slowly pulls the shirt over my shoulders and head, and then I look in the mirror at us.

She looks pale and horrified, a stark contrast to the ugly purple, boot-shaped bruises on my rib cage. Tears shimmer in her eyes, and she touches my skin with her fingertips. "Oh my God," she says. "Savage."

"I'm all right," I assure her. "Back when I was training for Ranger school, I fell off a twenty-foot-high wall. Landed right on my side because I wasn't all the way... Thank fuck. Thought I pierced a lung, but it was just some really screwed-up ribs. This isn't even that bad."

"You were in the army?" she asks, her fingers soft and cool against my hot skin.

I nod. "Conversation for another day."

I unbuckle my belt, but shimmying out of my jeans is another story. Every twist of my torso and bend of my waist sends waves of pain through my body.

"I can do that," she says quietly.

"I want a woman to want to undress me." I try to make a joke of it, and she meets my eyes, her lips pressed into a grin.

"Oh, I want to," she teases.

I chuckle, but then I cough. "If this is what it's like to grow old with somebody," I say, "you didn't sign up for this shit."

Claire laughs at that and stands between me and the sink, her eyes on my hips. "I'm going to unzip you, okay? Then I will..." Her voice cracks a bit, like she's scared or at least uncomfortable.

I rest a hand on her shoulder. "Claire, I've never had

a woman undress me who wasn't begging to do the job." I shake my head. "I can handle it from here."

"So, you want me to beg?" Her voice lilts in an unmistakably flirtatious tone. "Because I'm not about to watch you crack your head open on the sink."

I groan. "All right, all right. But I'm commando under here, so just…" I plant a hand on the edge of the sink. "Unzip me, shove these down just a bit, and…"

"Savage." Claire is pinned between me and the sink, and she rests one of her palms against my chest. "I have a baby. I hope you don't think I've never seen a dick before."

A laugh rumbles low in my chest. "Yeah, but the first time you set eyes on my dick, I want it to be a lot sexier. Now unzip me and skedaddle."

She mutters "skedaddle" under her breath, but she does as I ask. She works the zipper of my jeans down and then wriggles the waistband onto my hip bones.

"Come running if you hear me drop," I tell her.

"You going to drop the shampoo on purpose?" she asks. "Because I'm right here, right now, and if you want me to see the goods…"

"No goods." I take hold of her chin and raise her face to meet my eyes. "Claire," I say, my voice going serious. "That's as much of my junk as I'm ready to share. Now get the hell out of here and leave a man with his dignity, will you?"

She purses her pretty lips and shakes her head, but she steps outside of the bathroom. "I'm leaving the door open," she calls behind her.

I grin and carefully step into the shower. I'm only thirty-seven, but I feel every minute of those years all the way down to my bones as the hot water crashes down on my skin.

My face hurts.

My head hurts.

My neck hurts.

My goddamn everything hurts.

I can't reach up to shampoo my hair, but I wash the goods, rinse off, and wrap a towel around myself. The second I turn off the water and open the door, I hear Claire's voice.

"Be careful getting out of the shower."

I shake my head. "Yes, ma'am." I feel better being clean, but by no means do I feel okay. I step like my feet are made of lead onto the bathmat, and then I realize I didn't bring any clean clothes into the bathroom. "Fuck it. Claire?"

She opens the door so fast, it bangs against the bathroom wall. She jumps and her face pales. "I'm sorry," she says quickly. "I didn't mean to—"

"Don't apologize. I need you." I'm gripping the towel around my hips, but that's about all I've got in me. "I forgot clothes," I stammer, my words failing me as the pain from the exertion catches up to me. "But I've got to sit. I'm…"

"It's okay. Come on." Claire tucks herself under my armpit. "Just hang on to your towel. You're getting in my bed, and I don't want to hear any arguments."

I'm not about to fight her on this. I hobble with her

help to her bed, lower myself down, and lie back against the pillows, which she's moved from the couch. "I'm so sorry," I whisper through gritted teeth. "I should be more of a fucking man than this."

She covers my legs with the blankets and then, making sure nothing below the waist is exposed, she reaches for the corner of the towel and gently pulls it out from under me. "Savage," she says gently, wringing the towel between her hands. "Why would you apologize?"

I let my eyes fall closed. "Same reason you did," I mutter, and then I pass the fuck out again.

I spend the next few hours, or maybe it's days, in and out of consciousness. I am vaguely aware of Claire's presence, of a doctor coming to examine me, of swallowing down stronger pain meds and sips of soup, but most of the time, I'm completely out of it. It feels like days go by in a blur of stumbling to the bathroom to piss and taking pain meds. I know days pass only by how many times I wake up when it's light compared to dark.

When I finally open my eyes for more than a few pain-soaked minutes, again, it's dark in the room. I hear the distant whirring of a white noise machine and see the faint light of a laptop coming from across the room. I shift against the pillows and groan. "Claire?" I keep my voice low in case Aurora is sleeping.

I see the laptop light move and hear rustling from the couch. "I'm here," she says quietly. "How do you feel?"

I take a minute to really think about that. "Hungry," I chuckle. "When the fuck did I last eat anything?"

She clicks on a bedside lamp. "It's been a while," she says, her lips pulled down into a frown.

As my eyes adjust to the light, I realize I'm still in her room. "Shit," I mutter. "I'm still in your bed. How long has it been?" I scan the room and don't see a crib. "Where's Aurora?"

Claire sits on the edge of the bed beside my legs. I'm still naked under the covers, and I wonder how many times I've gotten up to piss and given her a hell of a show. No use worrying about that now.

"Phantom suggested we move Aurora into your room while you're here," she says quietly. "I have the monitors set up so I can be there in under five seconds if she wakes up." She smiles. "I'm just glad you don't have naked pictures of girls up on the walls."

I don't know whether to laugh or curse.

She nods, her eyes locked on mine. "I've been so worried," she says softly. She reaches out and strokes my hair back from my face. "You were talking in your sleep, and it seemed like you were having a nightmare."

"What did I say?" I ask, staring into her eyes.

"Savage…" She looks away, slowly pulling her hand from my hair.

"Claire." I grab her wrist lightly and move my

fingers to hers. I lock our fingers together and squeeze gently. "Please. Just tell me what I said."

She looks from my face to our fingers, but she doesn't move to pull away. Instead, she shocks the shit out of me by pulling my hand to her lips and kissing my knuckles. I feel tears fall from her eyes and drip onto our hands. "Let's just say I think I understand now why you saved me."

Neither one of us says anything. We hold hands, her tears wetting my knuckles. I don't know what to say. Thank you? I'm sorry? Fuck my old man for beating my mother, for beating me? Fuck guys like Anthony and Mad Dog, who use their fists instead of real strength?

"There's no fucking way on this earth I could have left you like I found you. But you took it, you took the hand I held out to you. Why didn't she? Why didn't my mom?"

Claire places her hand on me. "It doesn't mean she didn't love you. I promise you that, Savage."

"She feared him more than she loved me," I spit out. "That's the fucking truth."

"No." Claire cups my face in her hands and squeezes gently, which I appreciate because my jaw is still bruised. "Listen to me, Savage. Please." Her eyes are wild when I meet them. "She loved you more than she loved anything in the world, and that's why she stayed. She stayed to protect you. To put herself between him and you. That's how much she loved you. Enough to make a deal with the devil."

"I hope when he finally meets his maker, he rots in

hell," I grit out, my teeth chattering I'm so enraged. "Right next to Anthony and Mad Dog and all the rest of them."

Claire lowers her forehead to rest against mine. "You saved me," she whispers. "You're my salvation. And every minute of every day, you being alive, you being her son, that's what saved her. Even if you couldn't get her out, I promise you on my baby's life, you're her salvation too."

Claire leans forward and plants the softest kiss against my lips. I reach my hands behind her hair and hold her there, her forehead against mine. If I'm her salvation, then she might just be mine too.

EIGHT
CLAIRE

SAVAGE SPENDS the next week in my room, recovering from his injuries. During the day, I bring Aurora out to the front of the compound, and we play outside in the grass, practicing standing, reading books, or just talking to each other with Aurora's growing vocabulary of sounds that want to be words.

Most days, Savage hobbles his way into a lawn chair to watch. He and Tank have started a contest to see who can teach my daughter how to high-five faster.

So far, Tank's in the lead, but I don't think Savage really minds. He watches her play with a curious combination of amusement and interest on his face.

He keeps his distance, and I have to imagine—even though he hasn't said anything—that he feels a mixture of fear and responsibility when it comes to my daughter. If he was subjected to what I think he was as a child, I can't even imagine what watching my daughter brings up for him emotionally.

I can't help watching Savage. It's clear he has an important role here at the club. Bikers like Phantom, Shadow, and Viper consult with him all day, visiting him in my room or coming outside to talk in low voices.

I'm used to being a bystander when it comes to club business. Anthony's motto was always *what I didn't know couldn't hurt me*, and while I didn't love it, I'm grateful now that I don't carry guilt about whatever he was doing that cost him his life.

I try not to think too much about what the Heat does or does not do. The way I met them means they need guns. And that kind of information makes me sick with worry if I think about it too often. Just seeing how hurt Savage is and imagining the kinds of people who did that to him, it's enough to make me rethink my plan to steal a pair of shoes and run off the first chance I get.

It's funny, though. I have my own shoes now. The bruises around my eye have healed, and I could easily gather up my shit and walk out the front door.

I sincerely believe that the only reason anyone would stop me would be to ask if I need a ride somewhere. Maybe real power isn't in the running, but in knowing that I have the freedom to choose what I want. And day after day, I've been choosing to stay.

And every night when I tuck Aurora into her crib in Savage's room and fall into this delicious routine that's so sweet and comforting, it hardly seems real.

We climb on top of my covers and sit side by side, my head against his shoulder. We eat diner food or food that Stella and the other club girls cook on our laps. I show him videos from my mom's days headlining Neon Dawn, or we talk about my old job and my old life, the work I used to do before all the Anthony bullshit ended my career.

We don't talk about the hard stuff. How I convinced myself that Anthony's jabs and insults—both physical and verbal—were things I deserved. How he wedged his way into my life after my mom died so that there was no room for anything but my grief and his demands.

We don't talk about Savage's parents or his childhood, but I get the sense from the hints he's left that both of his parents are still alive. He does tell me a little about his military career, how he was dishonorably discharged and couldn't finish Ranger school.

His mom called him in a panic one day, thinking she needed to go to the emergency room. His mom never fully explained what happened, but when Savage got word that his mom was in bad shape, he left base and took the first flight home from Ranger school. That alone would have been enough to get him dishonorably discharged. But when he saw his mom doubled over and throwing up blood, he beat his father to within an inch of his life. That was twelve years ago. He got booted from the military, lost everything, and hasn't spoken to either of his parents since.

He's alone in life now, except for the Heat. In a weird way, so am I.

The white noise machine coming through the

monitor is making me feel drowsy and relaxed. I rest my head against his shoulder, grateful for the comfort it brings me. I think he likes it too, but tonight, he lifts his arm and rests it on my shoulders. The movement brings me closer to him, closer to his injured ribs.

I crave the comfort of his body in ways that I know I shouldn't. I try to resist, to hold my weight and lean away a little. "I don't want to hurt you," I say as I turn to face him.

His beautiful brown eyes spark as he looks down at me. "Nah, but it'd be worth it if you did. You cool with it?"

I shouldn't be cool with any of this. Shouldn't be cool cozying up to a man who bought my freedom, a man to whom I owe so much. But he's wearing a gray T-shirt that looks so soft and smells so inviting.

"I'm cool with it," I tell him. I snuggle against his side and take a deep breath in. I can't help myself. He smells so damn good.

We're quiet until the grainy video of Neon Dawn playing in a bar someplace outside of Buffalo, New York, back in the early nineties ends.

"Do you sing like your momma?" he asks, his voice rumbling through his chest and sending tendrils of pleasure through mine.

"Nuh-uh." I shake my head. "I don't know who my daddy was, but I bet I got his pipes. When I sing, it sounds like those videos of Siberian Huskies trying to talk." I chuckle. "I'm only glad Aurora is too young to care how bad I sound. Once she's old enough, she'll probably ask me to stop singing, even the happy birthday song."

"You hush," he says, his voice low and gravelly. "I bet you sound beautiful. Every bit of you, Claire. Even the parts you think are less than perfect. You're beautiful."

I shake my head. He can't mean it. "I'm not at all. I—"

"*Hush*," he interrupts. "And take the damn compliment, woman. You're a goddamn hottie. Any man in his right mind would be lucky to have you. It's only the shit-for-brains losers—no offense to Aurora's dad—who would think otherwise."

I giggle at that. "Anthony was a bit of a shit-for-brains loser."

Savage grows quiet. His breaths are slow and steady, and the rise and fall of his rib cage is soothing. I rest my cheek against his chest as he asks, "You ever miss him? He ain't been gone that long. I know it's got to hurt sometimes."

I take a deep breath. I don't even have to think about the answer. I know how I feel. "Missing him isn't something I think I can ever do," I say. "I know it sounds wrong, and it feels wrong to say, but he and I… We weren't together in an intimate way after I got pregnant. He got real weird after that positive pregnancy test. He wasn't much for talking. Punching and swearing, yeah. But talking… Not toward the end. I feel like he was an enforcer of rules—do this, be quiet, stop doing that—and not a boyfriend. At least, that's how the last couple of years went."

As I talk, Savage gently tightens the arm that's around my shoulders, pulling me closer. "I'm sorry," he says. "You loved him once, though?"

He says it like a question, and I wonder if he is asking because he's thinking about his mom. How any woman could love a man who hurts her.

"I did." I nod, and my long, loose hair rubs against his shirt. I close my eyes and breathe in his scent, my cheek resting against his muscled chest. "But love means different things at different times. In the beginning, it can be sex, need, or passion, and then it changes."

"Your mom ever marry anybody?" he asks.

"Oh, hell yeah. My mom was no stranger to a marriage license. She used to joke that everybody needs a starter husband before they're ready for the forever man." I laugh. "Turns out, Mom needed three starter husbands and an anonymous baby daddy. She never did find herself a forever man, but she definitely didn't mind. She used to say, 'I thought I married smarter each time, but baby, it's like these men pay for the rings in IQ points.'"

I start laughing then, really laughing, so hard that I turn around and kneel, facing Savage while I catch my breath. "My mom even bought her own ring with the last husband just to see if that kept him from going stupid." I've got tears in the corners of my eyes, and I can hardly catch my breath. "But we all know how that turned out. Momma had a ring, a dent in her bank account, and a man who was still dumber than a box of rocks."

Savage is grinning so huge, he's showing all his perfect white teeth. God, he's pretty. For a former soldier and a bad-ass biker, he's beautiful through and through. That thought sobers me up a bit, and a question occurs to me.

"Why do you call yourself Savage?" I cock my head to one side and lazily run my fingers over the knees of his black sweatpants.

He grunts, and I wonder if I've hit a nerve.

"Never mind," I say, waving my hands in the air. "You don't have to—"

"It's all right." He rubs underneath one eye and I'm wondering if he's tearing up, but he's not. He's staring down at my hands. "When I was a kid, any time my dad got in one of his moods, he'd scream, 'What the fuck is wrong with you? I ain't raising no savages.'" He lifts his chin and looks me square in the face, and my heart thuds harder. He's so gorgeous, and the honesty and vulnerability in his voice make me feel raw inside. "My real name's Ethan. Ethan Everett. But I left that name behind the day I chose to become the very thing my daddy never wanted me to be—a savage."

I swallow hard and weigh my next words carefully. "Seems like the joke's on him, then," I say. "You are Savage if you think about it. You're fierce and wild. Untamed. Good in every way. From what I've heard, he was never kind and loving, caring and considerate. He never raised you to be any of those things, and that's exactly what you are. At least, that's how you've been to me."

I meet his eyes, and the next thing I know, he reaches for my hand. "Come here," he says softly.

I crawl back toward the top of the bed and kneel beside his legs, facing him.

"Is that what you think of me?" he whispers. Our heads are lowered, and I can feel the soft rasp of his callused hand against my cheek.

"I believe that about you," I say, correcting him. "And more, Savage. So much more."

His hand slides from my cheek to underneath my hair. He cups the back of my neck. "Claire…" My name on his lips sounds like music, like the prettiest song I've heard in a long, long time. "I've been wanting… I don't want you to feel like you have to… I…"

I stop his stammering with a finger over his lips. "Savage, I want to kiss you more than I want to breathe."

He swallows so hard his lips tense beneath my fingers. Then he takes the hand that's behind my neck and pulls me close to him. I lick my lower lip, excitement flaring deep in my belly. At the same time, my heart is racing. Once I kiss this man… If I kiss this man… How will that change what he is? What he wants?

I don't have time to worry because I feel his nose nudge mine. I lift my face, so close to his I can see the dark, rich chocolate of his brown eyes. He's so beautiful. Thick lashes frame his eyes, and his stubble rakes across the tender skin of my fingertips… Oh God. I'm holding his face, stroking the sharp edges of his jaw with my thumbs. My breathing catches in my chest, and I swallow.

"Claire." My name is on his lips. The soft puffs of his breath tease my lips, and I lick them again, my eyelids fluttering shut. The heat of his large hands on the back of my neck radiates down my back, and I arch toward him, knowing that what we're about to do will change everything. I wish my brain could process thoughts, could protect me or stop me, but something stronger than my mind and more powerful than my fear takes hold.

"Savage," I whisper back, and then it's me who's making the first move. It's my tongue that licks across his thick lower lip. It's my gasp at the electricity that flares between us when I feel that soft, plump flesh under my tongue. He tastes…so good. So sweet. I swallow and open my eyes, my lids feeling heavy and soft all at the same time. "Savage, please…"

I want him to want this as much as I do, and he answers my plea with his lips. He's leaning forward on the bed, my neck cupped in his firm hands, his mouth covering mine.

"Fuck…" he groans against my lips, "Fuck me, Claire, you're so…so…"

But his words disappear when I open my mouth. The gentle press of his lips against mine transforms into something deeper, something so real, so powerful, everything in my world narrows to him. His tongue sweeping my mouth. His lips claiming mine, tasting me, exploring every part of my mouth with such hunger that our teeth clack together.

"On my lap?" His words are a question, an invitation. One that I feel able to accept or decline—he's giving the power of what this becomes over to me.

I answer it without hesitation. He moves the laptop to the bedside table, and I climb onto his lap, my knees bent so I can run my hands along the perfectly shaped muscles of his shoulders as I kiss him. A welcoming heat pools between my legs, and my belly feels full and hungry all at once. I kiss him, tasting his mouth, working my fingers along the fabric of his T-shirt. It's like my hands have never touched anything so perfect, so fascinating. I can't decide what to touch and where to feel him because everything—the long waves of his hair, the rough outgrowth of stubble on his face, the arms that are so strong but hold me with perfect pressure against him…I want it all. I can't believe how he feels and that he's real. But he's here and I want this. I want him.

I kiss him deeper, and I can't help the tiny moans of pleasure, the needy, arousal-soaked gasps that slip between my lips every time we pause for air. I pull away from his mouth and tenderly kiss his chin, the still-bruised jaw that's got to be sore. I run my fingers through his hair, scratching his scalp lightly with my nails and tugging his face closer to mine when I bring my lips back to his.

We take turns exploring each other's mouths, but his hands seem frozen in place, while mine are touching everything—his shoulders, his arms, his head. I pull back, my nostrils flaring as I try to drink in every scent of him—his cologne, his soap, the natural scent of his skin.

"Savage, what's wrong?" I whisper. I look down at his hands. They're planted like statues on my hips. I can feel his arousal, thick and hard, springing up between us, so I don't think it's that he isn't attracted to me.

"I want you so goddamn bad," he grunts, his eyes flaring with sparks of honesty and something else, some emotion I can't place. "You don't have to do this, Claire. I…"

"Is that what you think?" I pull my hands back to myself and lean a little farther back so we can look each other in the eye. "That I'm paying you back?"

My body grows cold, and I move to get up off his lap, when his hands clamp down harder.

"No. Fuck no. That's…well, yeah. That's what I'm afraid of. You don't owe me this, Claire."

I guess we were gonna have to have this conversation eventually. I look over at the baby monitor. The white noise machine in Aurora's room is soft and steady, and I can see in the color image that she's sound asleep, peacefully dreaming. Her little mouth is open, and she looks healthy. Cared for. Safe.

I point at it. "You gave me and my daughter everything when we had nothing. When I was nothing. I'm still nothing," I tell him. "I have nothing to give you but what's in here." I hold a hand over my heart. "And this." I lean forward and kiss him lightly, then pull back and meet his eyes. "Is that enough for you, Savage? Am I enough for you? Scars and all?"

"Fuck yes," he hisses, no hesitation in his answer. "But if we do this, if we go where I sure as fuck want to go, it will change everything. Can you handle that?"

I shrug. "I don't know," I tell him honestly. "But can you say for sure that you can handle it? Maybe we're two broken pieces that, together, make a whole. I don't know. You can't know either, not now. But if I tell you I want you, I want this—at least for right now—is that enough?"

"More than enough," he growls.

I don't know if this is the worst decision I've ever made or the only good one. But my brain is still turned off, and my fears are caged like the pounding of my demanding heart. Savage is a good man. He hasn't hurt me. I've never seen him hurt anyone—except maybe the assholes who roughed him up. Even before Anthony, I knew that life didn't come with a guarantee. A promise of sunshine and rainbows and happily ever after.

But I'd have to be dead in the ground not to want this—this man, this chance—the hope of something that maybe isn't perfect. But that's enough. Maybe even more than enough.

"Kiss me, Savage," I beg him. "And don't hold back. At least for tonight, I'm yours."

NINE

SAVAGE

She's mine. She's mine.

The words echo through my mind for about a second before I claim her, take what I realize I've been wanting since her first shower in this room. Since she opened those wide green eyes and accidentally called me babe. And yet somehow, even back then, that felt right. It felt inevitable.

I free my hands from their self-imposed prison and give myself permission to touch her. To hold her. I cup Claire's face in both hands and bring her lips to mine. I'm tasting her, losing myself in her sweetness and her spice, fisting her hair lightly and savoring every gasp and murmur that passes from her lips to mine.

I still haven't healed all the way, so my rib cage

starts to burn, but I don't care. There is no way I'm gonna stop now. She's given herself to me, and I don't know yet how far we will take this, but if all I have is tonight, I'm gonna take what she's willing to give.

I slide my hands from her face, wind my fingers through her hair again, and then move my hands down to the hem of her sleep tee. She's dressed for bed, braless and in pajama shorts, and the smooth lines of her thighs make my mouth water more than the plush lips that kiss me back with a fervor that matches mine.

I'm used to women wanting to fuck me, but this feels different. This feels like more. Claire cared for me. Smoothed back my hair when I was sleeping, fed me pain meds and water when I was too weak to hold up my own head. Between every kiss and touch, she's looking at me like she fucking cares. Like the shit I've shared with her isn't some black mark on my soul that drives her away. Instead, it's a thing we share, a bond of something we both understand so deeply, it's like we're cut from two parts of the same cloth.

"Claire," I murmur, my fingers skimming the soft flesh under the hem of her shirt. "Can I—"

She cuts me off. "Anything. Yes to all of it, Savage."

I waste no time taking what I want, but I'm not gonna be a fucking animal about it. If Claire is offering herself to me, then I'm gonna take the gift she's giving and treat it the way she deserves to be treated. The way I'm gonna guess she hasn't been treated in too long.

I slowly tug the top up and over her shoulders. She

helps me work her arms out and then sits before me on the bed, her breasts firm and small but surprisingly full. Her skin pebbles, and her nipples grow hard as I watch the pink peaks. Long chestnut-brown hair falls down her back, and she parts her lips, her lids half lowered. She sucks her lower lip into her mouth and takes a long, slow breath, her chest rising and falling with the action. It's like a siren's call, and I can't hold myself back.

I awkwardly pivot from where I'm sitting with my back against the headboard and lay her down on top of the covers. It's my turn to kneel as she lies back, and I just look at every inch of her. The faded yellow bruises are gone, her belly is soft, and her tits… God, my mouth fucking waters as I decide where and how to touch her first.

I run my fingers along her bare arms, watching as her toes curl and her eyes close on a sweet, seductive sigh. Her breathing is steady, and I run my hands along her hands, lace my fingers through hers and squeeze, before moving to the sides of her ribs. I pass my hot hand over her breast, and she sucks air so fast I freeze. I keep going when she smiles and murmurs, "That's so good. Don't stop."

Her nipples are soft and light pink. I trace a circle with my fingertips, drawing long strokes around her fullness until she whimpers and flexes her thighs.

"More?" I ask. "What do you like, baby?"

I want to hear her voice, confident, demanding. I want her to tell me what she wants and how she likes to be touched. I want to know exactly how to please her, so I can give her everything she's ever wanted and more.

"Suck me, squeeze me," she says, her voice shaking.

I obey, lowering my hand and taking her tender nipples between my fingertips. I squeeze lightly, tugging the flesh toward me and watching as her entire body reacts. I tug and twist, slowly and softly at first, but then I work her nipples harder until the delicate skin is flushed a rosy red.

She gasps, gripping the sheets in her fingers. A cherry-colored blush blossoms on her chest, and her cheeks go pink. Her mouth is open, she's licking her lips, and she's working her hips in little squirming motions.

Every movement she makes sends bolts of heat to my cock, and before I know it, I'm so hard, I'm afraid I'm gonna split the seam of my sweatpants.

I am nowhere near ready to fuck this woman, no matter what my body demands, but I can't wait a second longer to taste her. I lower myself carefully, holding back a stream of curses at the pain in my ribs, and straddle her thighs. I bend forward at the waist and kiss her breastbone, using my fingers to keep the pressure on her nipples.

She sighs at my kiss, but then a ragged spike shoots through my side. I roll off her and crash onto the mattress, facing the ceiling. "Nope," I say through a laugh. "That ain't happening."

Her eyes fly open, and she grabs for her sleep shirt to cover herself. "What happened?" she asks, her voice worried.

"Ribs ain't liking that. So, I'm gonna need your help, baby. We gotta trade places."

She grins and drops the sleep shirt.

I lie back against the headboard again and pat my thighs. "Here," I tell her.

She straddles me, and I pull her close, then scoot my ass a little lower on the bed so I can cup her tits in my hands and bring them close to my face.

I give her no warning, I just lick one hard nipple up and down, laving the tender flesh with my tongue while holding her hips in my hands.

She gasps and arches her back, pressing into my chest. I feel her fingers weave through my hair, and she feeds me her tit, urging me to take her fully into my mouth.

I happily oblige, sucking her nipple all the way into my mouth hard, then soft. I nibble it and breathe hot kisses on the underside of her breast, worshipping every inch of her skin until she's trembling with need.

"Savage," she cries softly, "my God, that feels so good."

"How good?" I ask her, blowing a warm breath along her flushed breast. "What do you need, baby?"

"More," she pants. "I just want more."

"We gotta get up," I tell her because I'm in pain again.

She widens her eyes but scoots off my lap. I roll off

the bed and take her hand, then in one swoop, I tug her sleep shorts and panties off. She stands beside the bed, her breasts pink from my attention, from my mouth. Her thighs tremble with desire, and I resist the urge to stop and taste every freckle that dances a path from her knees to her hips.

The sight of her bare thighs, the curls of her hair covering her pussy, makes me painfully hard. But I motion for her to lie back on the bed, and she does, settling herself so her ass is at the edge of the mattress. I'm gonna make sure she gets every bit of satisfaction she needs. This will do the job. As long as I don't have to twist my torso too much, I can make this work.

I kneel on the floor and rake my hands up and down her thighs. She sighs and shudders as I massage my way from her knees to her hips and down again, widening her legs apart when I get back to her knees.

From this vantage point, I can bend just a little and see every inch of her pussy, spread open for me and fucking wet. It takes every ounce of my self-control to keep my dick in my pants, every bit of restraint I possess not to plunge myself deep inside and fuck her senseless.

Not yet.

Not yet.

Not yet.

First, I take a finger and stroke her, moving past her damp curls and finding her core. She whimpers and squirms but widens her legs farther, giving me an even better view of her pleasure. I stroke her wetness and spread it everywhere, paying special attention to her swollen clit. I can't fucking help myself, though. I stop and pull my fingers away, sticking them in my mouth to suck her juices off my fingertips.

"Sweet as fucking sin," I whisper, licking my fingers clean. "My God, baby, you're delicious inside and out."

She giggles and grips the bedsheets in her fingers. "Savage, fuck…"

"I know, baby. I know." I go back to her pussy, stroking her and lightly tapping her clit just to get it wet. Then I gently pinch the swollen bud between two fingers and roll her moisture over it, kneading her sensitive flesh to work up the pleasure until she's writhing and panting.

"Savage," she gasps, grabbing for my hair and tugging, pushing, wriggling for me to release the same ache I know I'm feeling.

"I got you," I promise. Then I slide one finger inside her, reaching deep and crooking until I feel the spongy wall deep inside. I lower my mouth and let my tongue take over the work on her clit while one finger, then two, explores her hot, wet center.

"Oh no, no, no," she groans, her hips bucking, lifting and riding to meet my hand. "Oh God, no, this is too good. Savage, I can't… Savage, I'm gonna…"

I hum my satisfaction against her sweet pussy, then roll the tip of my tongue over her clit while finger-fucking her hard and deep. "Come for me, Claire. Come on, baby."

At my words, she melts, releasing a high-pitched

moan that has me leaking inside my sweats. "Oh fuck, Savage."

Then I feel it, the clenching of her walls, the euphoric spasm as she lifts her hips and grabs my hand with hers, grinding against my fingers as she wrings every ounce of pleasure from my touch.

"That good, baby?" I ask. "You want more?"

"More," she begs, her voice a cry and a squeak, a prayer and a song all in one.

"We good to go bare?" I ask.

She gasps a little at my question but says, "Yeah. Yes. God, yes, just fuck me, Savage."

She's barely through her first orgasm when I lower my sweats and line up the tip of my cock against her. I drag the head through her curls, making sure I'm good and wet.

"Oh my God," she groans and then opens her legs even wider, holding her knees with her hands.

I hear nothing but the crash of blood in my ears at that point because my cock slides inside Claire like I was made to fit her. I'm balls deep before I realize it, and her walls tighten down on me, clamping. I have to hold her knees and go still, or I'm gonna blow before I even have the chance to fuck her.

I catch my breath and open my eyes, watching as I rock my hips, and my dick slides in and out of the most beautiful woman I've ever seen, the strongest, most intense, most amazing woman to ever come into my life. I go as slow as I can, trying to savor every single whimper, every single moan.

But then I lose myself.

Lose all thought.

I rock harder, thrust faster. Her tits bounce, she locks her fingers against her knees, and I fuck my way through the pain, through the pleasure, through every ounce of desire, fear, confusion, and protective feeling I've had since I laid eyes on Claire.

I fuck her so hard, we move the bed, we bang the headboard, and we're both crying out to God above for more. When I feel her clamp down on me, I give in.

Give in to the fucking bliss, to the darkness behind my eyes and the light in my heart. I come hard, my knees trembling, sweat dripping down my forehead and splashing on Claire's open thighs.

I come with a roar and a bliss so complete, it's the first time, the only time, I can ever remember feeling anything like this.

She didn't lie.

She's mine.

Completely.

Not just for tonight.

I can never let her go.

She's mine now and for fucking ever.

When I wake up, there is an empty space in the bed beside me and a hollow gnawing in my gut.

I spent the night—the entire night—tangled up beside Claire, her legs between mine, my hand cupping her breast, her hair splayed out around our pillows.

It was good. Too good.

Better than I've felt in weeks with these damn injuries, but better than I've felt in years with another human being beside me.

There is something about Claire that fits.

That just makes sense.

Being without her right now feels wrong, and I squint against the daylight and wonder where she went.

The white noise machine in my room, the one that soothes Aurora to sleep, has gone silent. I peek at the monitor, and I see Claire rocking Aurora in her arms.

"Good morning, baby," she says. Claire has put back on her sleep tee and shorts, and just seeing her body in the full-color image on the monitor makes my cock wake up. She sways as she holds her sleepy baby to her chest, humming a song I don't recognize. When she starts singing softly, I have to hold back a laugh.

She wasn't wrong about her singing. She's no Neon Dawn. But I could listen to her voice and watch her love on her baby for the rest of my life and never get tired of it.

I register the feeling as soon as I feel it, and something inside me tenses.

Last night unfolds in a series of images. Claire's pussy open to me, wet, and wanting. The long lines of her thighs trembling as she comes.

Then I remember what I did, fucking her until I was

senseless, boneless, my cock deep inside her with no fucking protection. We only fucked once, but I blew my load so deep inside that woman that she could probably see my come behind her eyes.

A sour taste fills my mouth. What the fuck is wrong with me? I never take risks like that. Never. But Claire has me out of my mind and not acting remotely close to my normal self.

Protecting them from Mad Dog was easy. I saw a problem, I had the power and the means to step in, and bam—I provided a solution.

But I'm a fucking mess of a man. I run guns, drugs, and collect gambling debts from scumbags. Right now, I'm nursing the bruising of the year, thanks to some assholes who thought they were just smart enough to outsmart the Heat.

I'm the fucked-up kid who took his daddy's fists and cried into his pillow. I lost my military benefits, my career, my dignity. I've got no mother, no family, and I am sure as fuck not ready to be any kind of father. I can't—no, worse, I don't want to do this.

It's not about Claire and what I feel for her. If it were just Claire, it would be hard enough to justify holding a beautiful, caring woman back from her potential by keeping her for myself.

I'm a criminal, a failure, a wreck.

And just about every day of the week, I put myself in harm's way. Anything can go down at any time, and it often does.

It's so much easier with no attachments.

No one to count on me for more than a night.

No one to need more than I have to give.

I jump out of her bed, my heart hammering in my chest, and my palms become clammy. What if I got her pregnant?

What if—

Fuck.

"Savage?" Claire's soft voice breaks me from my spiraling thoughts. She's cuddling Aurora to her chest, a soft smile on her face. Her eyes flick to my soft cock bobbing against my bare thighs. "Everything okay?" she asks.

But she can tell right away that everything isn't okay.

She points to where my sweats are pooled on the floor. "Why don't you put those on real quick, and I'll change Aurora's diaper. Okay?"

Her voice is soothing, but it's as if I can't move. I'm frozen, looking at her, the baby, and thinking thoughts that I never dreamed I'd think. What if I just made myself a daddy?

What if I—

"Savage." Claire's voice is firm now. "Sweetheart, would you mind just bending down and grabbing those sweatpants off the floor?"

I shake my head to clear the fog a bit and give myself over to her voice.

"There we go." She's talking to Aurora now, but for a second, I thought she was talking to me.

She's calm and composed but authoritative. Like

this is what I need to do, this is how it's gonna be, and like the good soldier I once was, I know a commanding officer when I hear one.

I do as she says and step into my pants.

"All right now. Why don't you sit down?"

I drop onto the bed.

She smiles and shakes her head. "Come to the couch, Savage. I'm gonna change Aurora and get her some breakfast." Claire moves quickly and quietly, talking in a low voice to her baby.

I sit back against the couch cushions and let my head drop back. I close my eyes and let the memories take over.

I ain't raising no savages!

You're a fucking worthless shit, boy. You know that?

What the fuck're ya crying for?

Little asshole.

Mama's boy. Ain't nothing ever gonna come of a shithead like you.

The voice crowds my ears, and I cover them with my hands.

Fuck him.

Fuck him.

Fuck my old man.

The adult in me, the mature man who's beaten, shot, and stolen to survive, takes over.

I'm powerful.

I'm strong.

He can't hurt me.

Not anymore.

I open my eyes at the feel of tiny fingers tugging on the ankle of my pant leg. I go bug-eyed at little Aurora. She's got the end of a baby bottle gripped between tiny budding teeth, and her hands are covered in drool and God only knows what. She's leaving wet marks on my sweats, and she's babbling behind her bottle.

"Maamaa maaa maaa, maaa maaa."

A fist closes around my heart, and I watch as she crawls around my feet, tugging at my pant leg.

I can't look at her.

I can't face this.

All I can picture is the kid I once was, vulnerable and soft and innocent like her.

And then I see the fucker who hated me so much, who had so much rage inside him that he looked at a vulnerable kid—maybe not a baby like Aurora, but a three-year-old, a five-year-old, a ten-year-old—and laid hands on him.

Fists.

Boots.

Whatever was within reach.

I swallow back the memories and the rage as I look into those crystal-blue baby eyes.

"How?" I whisper through the haze of my past. "How could he not fucking love me?"

Claire is dabbing at her eyes, watching her baby crawl around my bare toes. "He did, baby," she assures me, her eyes reddening with tears. "He hated himself, that's all. And he took that all out on you. You're not him. You're not filled with hate. You're filled with so much more. Love and kindness. I know what I'm talking about, Savage. He hated himself, but it was so much easier to act like he hated you."

I bend at the waist and stifle the curse of pain that reminds me my ribs are still fucked up. I look into little Aurora's eyes. I see Grandma Dawn, the woman I've spent the last week watching on YouTube with Claire, in her coloring. I see Claire in her round cheeks and pointed chin. I know Anthony is there too, but I refuse to see him. Refuse to see anything but love, innocence, patience, and sweetness.

"Maa-maaa?" Aurora takes the bottle of formula out of her mouth and holds it up to me. She can't walk yet, so I'm not sure what she wants me to do. I look to Claire for guidance.

"Do you want to hold her?" she asks. Her voice is a whisper, restrained emotion making the words come out slow and thin.

I shake my head. "No. No fucking way."

But then Aurora blows a huge raspberry of formula, and a bubble pops, spraying spit and milk onto her face. She laughs, and her wet little face curves into such a picture of sweetness that I swear to fuck, my heart stops in my chest.

How can I say no to this?

To her?

To them?

The same universe that gave me an old man who hated me, who took out every anger and complaint on me and my mother, has delivered Claire and Aurora literally to my doorstep. Maybe they aren't part of a fucked-up cycle that tumbles me back and forth, round and round.

Maybe they are something totally different and new.

A fresh start. A new beginning.

Aurora's giggle subsides, and she drops the bottle on the floor. She goes to pick it up, but I scoop it up before she can put the nipple back in her mouth.

"You got a clean one?" I nod at Claire. "Just in case that touched the floor."

"I've got a clean one," she assures me.

I make my decision right there. It's not rational. It's not sane. I don't even think it's intentional or conscious. Her bottle in one hand, I lean down and scoop up Aurora with the other. I pass the bottle to Claire, and she changes the dirty nipple out for a clean one. She hands the bottle back to me and I hand it to Aurora, but she takes it from my hand and tosses it on the floor.

"Aw shit," I say. "We're gonna need another nipple."

"I know the feeling," Claire grumbles over a wry smile.

I'm looking at her when I feel a chubby and surprisingly strong little hand grab on to one of my fingers.

"Mama." Aurora's babbling. "Mamaaaa." She's got my finger in a death grip. Then, before I know what to think, Aurora's resting her warm, soft head against my chest and pulling my finger to her mouth.

"She might be teething," Claire warns, picking up the bottle from the floor. She rests a hand on my thigh and smiles into my face. "But she won't break the skin if she bites you."

The tears that burn aren't from Aurora's little teeth hurting my finger. They're from Aurora's little face, her crystal-blue eyes, her laughter, and her mother breaking down the walls around my heart. I hold on to the little kiddo like I'll never let go.

TEN
CLAIRE

I'M FINE. Fine. Totally fine. Or at least that's what I keep telling myself. You would think having sex with Savage would have my heart in tangles and my nerves frayed like live wires, but watching Savage hold my baby does something painful and somehow perfect to me all at the same time.

I haven't trusted anyone with her. No babysitters until Poppy's daughters just a few days ago.

She's all I have left. My flesh, blood, yes. But more than that, Aurora is my heart. She's a living, breathing piece of my mama, the dad I never knew, and now, the father she'll never know.

I even named Aurora after my mother Dawn. Aurora, like the lights in the sky that bring hope even through the darkness. Mama and Aurora share those crystal-blue eyes, and now she's in the lap of a man I hardly know. She's resting her head against his chest, biting his fingers.

And I'm not afraid.

I'm not comfortable, not entirely, because old habits die hard, but I'm not afraid. Not of Savage. Not of this.

I watch them together as I gather up my clothes, and I wonder if Savage has any experience with a baby.

"What does she like to do?" His question is sincere, and he's looking at her with something like love on his face.

I mean, Aurora is such a sweet baby, it's impossible not to love her. But still, seeing the way he looks at her heals something I never thought could be fixed.

"At her age, she should be crawling and exploring. She loves her train." I take her pink-and-purple train and choo-choo it all the way up Savage's pant leg, making it do a little spin on his knee. He watches intently as I play with Aurora, teasing her, making silly noises. And then he takes the train from me and makes a deep, realistic engine sound.

Aurora grabs for the train excitedly.

I watch him with her and slowly relax. I sit on the floor cross-legged watching them play together, conscious with every movement of my body that I'm sore from the way he touched me, but not in a painful way. The pleasurable ache that makes me miss his hands on me and his mouth.

But he can't possibly have real feelings for me. What happened last night was an itch, right? A mutual scratch after the time we've spent together.

The idea makes me sad. I'm getting used to his deep brown eyes, the sadness and depth reflected there. His sculpted arms and heavy tattoos. I want to hold him and listen to every secret inked along his body and inside his heart.

Somehow, the man who bought my freedom got a piece of my heart as part of the deal.

But I know I can't hope for anything more than what I have already. A warm bed. A full belly. A roof over my head and respect as long as I'm inside these walls. He's been good to me, and I don't want to mistake that for more.

As I stand to grab a few snacks for Aurora, something occurs to me.

"Savage," I say quietly. He's whistling like a train, and Aurora is back to biting his finger. "I, uh... I haven't had a period in months. I don't know if it's stress or something else. I nursed Aurora for a bit, but it's never come back. So, last night..."

I hope he understands that, despite what we did, there's no way I can get pregnant.

His eyes meet mine, and I see an entire highlight reel of thoughts cross over his face. At first, discomfort. Then, confusion. Understanding, relief. I don't know.

He gives me a stiff nod and then scratches his head. "Okay," he says quietly, but then he chirps, "Ow."

Aurora pulls her mouth from his finger and laughs. That belly-deep, dimples-out baby laugh that always makes me smile.

"That really hurt. She's like a puppy, nipping and biting." He cocks his chin at her, but then a full grin overtakes her face. "She's so damned cute, Claire. She's so beautiful."

I nod. And it means a lot to me that he sees it too. I go over to him and hold out my arms, and as I knew she would, Aurora practically throws her body at me.

I take her from Savage and pat her back, rocking instinctively on my heels. "Go ahead and get coffee or some breakfast for yourself," I tell him. "Thanks for a special night. We'll be okay."

I want him to know that he doesn't have to stay here. We're not playing house. I get what this is and what it can never be. But damn if it doesn't hurt when he stands up, grabs his T-shirt from my floor, and balls it up between his hands. His feet are bare, and the muscles in his arms flex as he kneads the T-shirt between his long, tattooed fingers.

"All right." He pinches the bridge of his nose, and his mouth opens as if he wants to say more, but he looks from me to Aurora and back to me, and then he's gone.

By the time Aurora and I are ready to face the day, she is fussy. I feel her gums and they seem okay, but I wonder if she's starting to teethe. I try to play with her, but we're both in a mood. I don't want to admit that I'm thinking about Savage and last night. We've been through a lot together in the seven and a half months she's been alive.

Maybe I need to get out of this room where all I see is Savage, his naked body above me, his hands holding my knees open. I have to stop replaying the images and get something productive done today.

Feeling bold, I wander into the front of the compound.

"Well, well, well, look at you." Stella is yawning behind the bar, a giant travel mug in one hand. "The prettiest lady and baby in this den of thieves." She smiles at me and gives Aurora a wave.

"Morning, Stella." I walk up to the bar and set Aurora on my hip.

"You want something? Coffee? Whiskey for the little one?" Stella winks and I know she's teasing, but I shake my head and don't really laugh.

"I'm kind of in a mood today," I tell her. "I was hoping to go out someplace."

She nods. "You want company or a ride?"

I think about it. I have an idea where I want to go, and I think I'd like to be alone with my daughter. I packed the laptop in the diaper bag, and I have half a feeling that if I get something done today, I won't have this vague, nagging mood working its way through my belly. "A ride?" I say, more of a question than an answer. "You think someone would mind driving me?"

Stella shakes her head. "Hell no, he won't mind. He's in the garage with Viper."

I've never been in the garage, but Stella points the way, and I guess she expects me to go interrupt them and ask. My mouth goes sour for a minute, and I have a flashback to the Hellfires club.

These guys are not like that, I remind myself. *Stella wouldn't send me in there if it wasn't okay.*

I walk up to the door just off the kitchen and twist the knob. Inside, I see gleaming antique cars—sexy, old muscle cars, and vintage hot rods—motorcycles and regular cars, unlike the pickups the guys drive when they're not on their bikes.

I take it all in silently, but Viper turns the minute the door opens.

He nods at me, but his look isn't exactly friendly.

"I'm sorry," I stammer, "I…"

"Yo. Aurora." Tank waves and makes the high-five motion in the air. "You know what to do."

Aurora does not, however, know what to do, and she buries her face in my shoulder.

"Sorry to bother you," I say.

Viper spikes a dark brow up into his forehead and looks from me to Tank. "We're done here," he tells me, but it sounds like he just decided that. He turns, and the heels of his boots striking the pristine concrete floor of the garage make the hairs on my arms rise.

I'm uncomfortable interrupting these guys doing whatever they are doing. I'm uncomfortable asking for favors, but the sooner I get to finding a job, the sooner I can get out of all of their hair.

Viper passes by me, looking at Aurora like she's a contestant in the world's strangest animal contest, and then heads back into the compound. Tank saunters over to me.

"You need a driver today?" he asks.

"That depends," I tell him. "Will I be interrupting any big date plans?"

Tank frowns. "I don't think she's into me," he grumbles. "I think I've been fucking friend-zoned."

"You sure about that?" I ask. "You want to tell me what happened?"

He nods and heads out of the garage. As he passes me, he holds out his arm for my diaper bag. "I got that," he says. "Car seat is still in my truck. You know, it's funny, because..."

He's telling me about the girl he's seeing, but the minute we walk back into the compound, I feel a set of deep brown eyes on me. Savage is freshly showered, his hair is swept back from his face and tied down with a worn red bandana, and he's got well broken-in blue jeans on with a thin white tank top.

He watches me as I walk past him, his face an unreadable mask. I can't tell if he's angry or confused. And that just drives home the point even more.

I don't really know him.

But everything we shared comes crashing into my heart at full speed. I give him a thin smile, look away from his beautiful brown eyes, and follow Tank to the parking lot.

Neither one of us says a word.

I'm sitting at my usual table at the diner. I've got my laptop open, and I'm trying to tap away at the keys. How do you write a résumé when you don't have an address? I don't think anyone will know my phone is just a burner, but I don't honestly know. Is it a real number? If someone Googles it or Googles me, what will they find?

I sip my coffee and try to appease Aurora with smiles and cups of juice, but it's as if, today, absolutely nothing is going to be easy.

I have to bounce Aurora on my lap, let her crawl around in the booth, and finally, I have to get up and leave everything at the table and trust that no one will steal my stuff.

Aurora doesn't want to play or eat, and I don't think she's tired. I run a finger along her gums again, and I can feel a sharpness in one spot, but maybe my mind is playing tricks on me.

A thousand things run through my head. Maybe she's eaten something that doesn't agree with her and she's just not feeling right.

We've been through so many changes, and I'm alone for all of it. No mother. No sisters. No one.

I swallow back tears and rest my hand on Aurora's back. I try to soothe her and bounce her on my heels, but eventually, I look at her little face and ask, "What's wrong, baby? Mama just doesn't know what you need."

Thankfully, it's a late morning in the middle of the week, so there aren't too many people to witness our mini-meltdown.

Suddenly, I feel a light hand on my shoulder. "Honey, it looks like it's one of those days. Can I get you something?"

I turn and meet the face of Val, my now-favorite waitress. She's holding my diaper bag and a huge to-go bag.

She looks down at my things in her hand. "I hope you don't mind. I'm going on break soon, and I didn't trust that anyone else would look after your things. You hardly touched your breakfast, so I boxed it up, and I put a fresh cup of coffee in there." She smiles, a caring, wistful smile. "I just closed your laptop and slid it in the bag. I'm not very good with technology, so I hope I did it all right."

Hot tears burn behind my eyelids, and the tip of my nose stings. "Val," I say, "you didn't have to do that. Let me pay the bill, and I'll get—"

She interrupts me. "I took care of the bill. Your friend Savage there always tips me well. He tips me too much. He's a generous man, and any friend of his is somebody I'm gonna look out for."

I still have no clue why she thinks Tank is Savage. I've been meaning to ask, but it never feels like the right time.

"I can't let you do that," I say, holding back tears. Aurora is fussing again, and she wants to get down and crawl. I eye the filthy carpet and think I might just have to let her do it.

"It's done," Val says, setting my things down in a corner of the diner entryway. "Now don't think another thing of it. Just know that there are tough days for you, Mama, but that doesn't mean you're doing anything wrong. Sometimes, these little ones just don't know how to express everything they are going through." She smiles at Aurora. "Big thoughts and big feelings, the desire to get moving and grow up already. You just have to love them as best you can through the hard moments. That's all you can do."

Her words break a little at the end, and I know she's talking as much about herself as me. I want to ask if Val has kids and how old they are. I want to soak up any wisdom that she has to share, but then she nods, murmurs, "I'd better go take that break," and turns and leaves.

Tank shows up about ten minutes after I text him. "She's fussy today," I warn him. "It's probably a day for baby music."

He groans, but we listen to happy, upbeat music that seems to settle Aurora at least a little all the way back to the compound.

By the end of the day, I'm exhausted and crabby myself. I haven't seen Savage all day, and I plan on putting Aurora to bed, but moving the crib back to my room seems like a massive job to do alone. I feel like I've already imposed on people in the compound enough today.

Stella ran out to buy teething tablets for Aurora just

in case she is feeling some pain in her little gums. Tank, of course, drove me around, and even Shadow checked in on me earlier, knocking on the door to see if he could get me anything.

Apparently, Aurora's found her voice here with the Heat, because she was fussing so loudly, the bikers are probably completely over us being here.

Aurora seems exhausted by her normal bedtime, and I'm right there with her. A day of fussing and playing has us both on our last nerves.

I play one of her musical toys that has a soothing little ocean sound while I put her in fresh pajamas, and then I leave my room.

As soon as I step into the hallway, I see Savage. He's leaning against the wall, his eyebrows low. He looks from me to Aurora and doesn't say anything.

I'm too worn out emotionally from a day with the baby and the thousand confusing emotions warring in my chest to say anything.

I look up at him in question, and he nods, then steps aside to let us into his room.

When he looks from me to the baby, something big shifts on his face. A light comes into his whole body that I don't ever remember seeing before.

He practically relaxes, from his muscled shoulders to his clenched fists. He holds up a hand and waves at Aurora. "Hey, baby," he says. "Just came to say goodnight. From all my fingers except this one." He tugs on the index finger of his left hand, the one that

Aurora was biting on this morning. "This one's still holding a grudge."

I shake my head and chuckle, and Aurora babbles loudly as we walk past Savage. I tuck her into her crib, settling her in, and stroking her head. She must be wrung out from today. Her soft eyelashes cast little shadows on her cheeks, and she settles in to sleep much faster than I can believe. I click on the white noise machine and turn off the lights.

"I love you, baby," I whisper. "Tomorrow will be a better day."

I close the door and find Savage still standing outside the door of my room. He's looking down at his boots.

I want to ask Savage about his day. I want to tell him about mine. I need so desperately to share my life with this man. Not just anyone. Not Stella, not Tank. Not Poppy, who still texts me every other day, sometimes more.

I was alone in my relationship with Anthony for so long. Especially once I got pregnant. He wouldn't have been the kind of man I could curl up with on the couch and explain that Aurora had a bad day, that I'm tired and frustrated that I didn't know how to help her. That I'm worried I'm doing everything wrong. I want someone to share that with. Someone strong, someone who's been through real shit. Someone who won't judge me because he, too, doesn't want to sit on the receiving end of ill-informed judgment.

I hang my head and walk into my room, fighting the

loneliness, the fatigue, and everything else that makes me feel like an utter failure.

"Claire."

I turn at the sound of Savage's voice. I can barely lift my eyes to meet his, and I can't even summon a smile.

He doesn't say anything. Just opens his arms. "Come here," he demands, the order not cruel or selfish. The affection in his voice is so thick, I nearly burst into tears.

I do as he says, though. Even though I feel like a robot, my legs like lead, my head fuzzy with mixed-up messages, my body knows something more than I can comprehend. I go to him, lace my hands around his waist, and nestle my face against his collarbone.

He holds me tight, and we don't say anything, our mutual emotions—different as they must be—relaxing into the quiet peace of a hug.

Savage cups my face in his hands. "Claire." His whisper is gruff and deep.

He doesn't say anything else. Just lowers his face to mine, and an instinct, bigger and stronger and more powerful than my fears, my worries, my exhaustion, lifts my face to his.

Our kisses are soft at first. His lips tease mine, tasting, touching, pressing with such gentle sweetness, I want to remember these kisses forever. These are first-love kisses. First-everything kisses. The kind that makes the world around us collapse to nothing and every worry I have fade away.

I kiss him back, treasuring the feel of his strong jaw

under my fingers, the way I have to lift on my toes a little, and that brings my chest even closer to his.

I lean into him, into the kiss.

The breaths we trade, the gentle tapping of our noses. The kisses are slow, our lips exploring at a pace that feels curious and gentle, tentative and shy.

But then his fingers tighten on my hips, and I whimper, the sound slipping past my lips before I can stop it. He echoes it, but where my noise was small and strained, his is feral, needy, and raw.

He sweeps my mouth open with the tip of his tongue.

Then everything changes.

The air around us.

The energy that holds us together.

It shifts from an ember to a flame, and before I know what's happening, he's kicking my door shut and full-body carrying me to the bed.

He sets me down gently, and his eyes rove over my body. I'm fully clothed, but he's looking at me as if he's about to devour a feast that can never, ever satisfy his hunger. My insides liquefy as I watch him unbuckle his belt and toe out of his boots. He pulls a couple of foil-wrapped squares from the back pocket of his jeans, and I stifle a smile.

"Better safe than sorry?" I ask.

He shakes his head and unzips his jeans. His dick is already hard, its thick length pressing against the front of his navy boxer briefs.

"Safe," he says, working his jeans down his hips. "But never, ever sorry. Not when it comes to you."

He climbs into bed shirtless and with only his boxer briefs on. We look at each other for a minute, and he kneels beside me.

"I don't want just one night," he admits. His voice is low and quiet. "I want more. I just don't know how much more I can handle."

I nod. I understand. He doesn't have to say more. A lady with a past. A daughter from another man. I have no job, nothing to offer.

"I'm a lot to handle," I say with a small shrug. I close my eyes. "I know that, Savage. I know."

"No." He's got my hands in his, and he's pulling me close to him so we're both kneeling on the bed. "You're under my skin, Claire. I think about you constantly. I'm falling for you," he grits out. "And that's something I just can't do."

I squeeze his hands gently between mine. "I used to be good at a lot of things," I tell him, echoing the thing I tell myself when things look especially grim. "And I will be again someday. I don't need you to save me—more than you already have. I don't need you to raise my daughter. I just need your honesty. That's all."

He raises my hands to his lips and kisses my knuckles. "I want to taste every inch of you," he murmurs. "I want to love you so hard that you forget there was ever anyone else but me."

By love, I know he means fuck. So, I nod. "I want that too."

"And more," he tells me. "Claire, I want you to move in with me."

ELEVEN
SAVAGE

I LET the words come out of me, but I don't bother explaining. Something about holding Aurora, watching her crawl on the floor of this compound spare room. I don't know that I have space in my fractured heart to care for anyone for longer than a few nights, but I'm willing to try.

This woman cracks open every defense I have and sets every dark part of me loose.

And somehow, as much as I want to ride, as much as I want to pretend that everything that broke me is locked in a box where it can never hurt me again, she makes me face things, look at things. I can't explain it. It's like she's a storm that blew in on a soft breeze and she's shaking up everything I am.

She doesn't say anything in response to what I said, and I don't wait for her to speak. I reach for the cute little sleeveless thing she's wearing, and I untie the black bows on her shoulders. The ties fall down, exposing the straps of her bra, and I caress her bare shoulders, my thumbs working the delicate divots above her collarbones.

"You're so fucking beautiful," I tell her.

"I'm—"

"Don't," I tell her. Emotion sweeps over my heart. "I never want to hear you turn away a compliment I give you. I never want to hear you deny what I know about you. I see you, Claire. I see the love you have for your baby." I shove the bra straps off her shoulders while I talk. "I see the care you have for me. The respect you give everyone." I lean forward and plant hot kisses on her shoulders. "When I tell you you're beautiful, I want you to believe me. I want to make you forget every man who made you doubt that."

Both straps are down, and I tug the top of the fabric low enough that the tops of her breasts are exposed.

I was right to save Claire. To take her away from Mad Dog and the Hellfires and all the other shit that she went through in her old life. I'm also right to be careful what promises I make. What I give of myself. I'm damaged, and while some wounds heal, scars never go away. I'm not her hero, but I can help. That's all I can promise anybody. That's all I can promise her.

Her eyes flutter closed, and she has a sweet smile on her lips. I lay her back against the pillows and thank the heavens my ribs are healing day by day. I position myself beside her, fighting through the discomfort.

"Today was tough?" I ask, shoving the top of this one-piece outfit thing to her waist.

She squirms a little when her nipple hits the air. "My day is getting so much better now," she sighs.

I was wrong about Claire. Seeing her lying here, her eyes closed, her long hair tangled over the pillows, her nipples erect, and a small smile on her lips... She is the most beautiful woman I've ever seen. I've dated a lot of women, but I've never known someone's story, understood their past, and learned what matters to them before I took pleasure in their body.

Somehow, caring about Claire before we did this, seeing her so exposed, the vulnerability and the intensity all wrapped up in one stunning package, makes me so much harder.

It's like I want this woman on levels that I've never experienced before, and it's terrifying. Yet I'm powerless to stop it. I see her lips part, and the tip of her tongue darting over her lower lip to wet it sends my blood into a frenzy. All thought leaves my brain.

I lower my mouth to her breast and kiss my way around her hard nipples. I hover my palms over those tender peaks, not touching them, but teasing her with the heat of my hands and the hot flicks of my tongue along the fullness.

Her hands find my shoulders, stroking my skin while I kiss my way across her ribs. I breathe hot kisses against her belly, then reach my fingers back up to pinch her nipples and knead the flesh between the pads of my fingers.

She moans, and I work my mouth up to her neck,

thanking my ribs for cooperating with every pivot and shift of my body.

I kiss her neck, inhaling the combination of sugar and flowers, memorizing it. I move my hands from her breasts and grab her face, angling her toward me so I can kiss her lips.

She grabs my head and fists my hair, and we tear into each other's mouths, our breaths hot and fast, our lips pressing and brushing as we feast on each other with greedy need.

When I pull my mouth away from hers, I'm breathless.

I get off the bed, shove off my briefs, then climb back onto the bed, only for Claire to get up.

"Your turn," she tells me. She points at the pillows, so I lie back, my erection on full display.

She looks at it and smiles, then runs the palm of her hand along the side of my shaft. "You're the beautiful one," she says shyly.

She touches the underside of my cock, and a thousand white lights blast behind my eyes as pleasure rockets through me. Her touch is gentle until I feel her grasp the length of me. She nudges my legs open, then lies on her stomach between my legs, my dick in her hands.

I can't open my eyes, because I feel her hot breath against my cock and if I open my eyes and see her lips near my dick, I don't know that I'll be able to hold back.

My resolve is tested the second her lips press featherlight kisses along my erection. I feel her mouth everywhere. She caresses my balls in her hand and cups them with the perfect amount of pressure as she laps her tongue along the head of my cock. I suck in a breath and suppress a stream of curses.

She feels too good and too right.

She is unhurried, flattening her tongue along the sensitive underside. She strokes the surface of my balls, lightly scratching patterns against the skin, and I feel like I'm on a speed train to fucking ecstasy. I see light behind my closed eyes and feel every sensation as though it's the first time anybody sucked me off.

It's not, of course, but fuck, the way this woman takes her time. She acts like the only thing she has to do all night is lick me and suck me, and I'd be okay with that plan.

When she finally brings my entire cock into her mouth, she leans over me, her bare nipples hard, her hair hanging down, and I have to watch now.

As much as I want to get lost in the pleasure, to shut my eyes to everything in the world but this feeling, the more she sucks and the deeper she takes me, the closer I get to that cliff.

"Claire," I grit out. "Claire..."

She pulls her mouth from me, reaches toward the bedside table, and grabs one of the condoms I bought.

"Safe." She smiles and tears open the packet. She rolls the condom down my wet cock. She meets my eyes, her chestnut hair falling over one breast, a wicked, playful smile on her lips. "This is the very best way to end a rough day." She angles herself over me and then lowers herself inch by brutal inch.

She must be soaked because I slide in almost too fast, and she gasps and freezes, her thigh muscles tightening.

"Savage." Her eyes blaze, and I don't think my name has ever sounded so fuckin' sexy on any other woman's lips. In fact, she's ruined me for other women. The image of her rosy nipples, hard and firm, her long, wild hair, her lightly freckled thighs… Claire is ruining me, and all I want is more. All of it. All of her.

She tightens her pussy a little as she lowers herself, the tiniest little clench that squeezes the head of my cock. Another wave of intense pleasure washes over my weak limbs, and I lie there, her willing toy.

"Ride me, babe," I tell her. "Claire, I need you to fuck me, baby."

She lowers herself down until she's fully seated on my cock, and for a minute, it's as if she loses all her strength. She sags forward, her eyes shut and her hands around my face. She breathes kisses into my mouth, purring and whimpering. "You. Feel. So. Good."

I kiss her back, my dick reacting to her hot, sweet mouth and my cock deep inside her. I start to move my hips, needing more, needing her friction, but I force myself to stop.

She pulls her mouth from me and sits upright, her small, firm tits right at my eye level.

"Claire," I groan. "I need a framed picture of this. God, I could never get enough of this view."

She laughs and leans back, proving me immediately wrong. She tilts her hips and lifts off me, then sits back down so I have an almost unobstructed view of my cock disappearing inside her.

"Scratch that," I croak. "That's the sight. That's the view."

She smiles but closes her eyes and seats herself fully on top of me. Then she starts to rock her hips gently, back and forth. I reach for her tits, twisting her nipples between my fingers.

"Oh my God," she cries out. "Don't stop, Savage."

I have to close my eyes, because God help me, I'm not gonna last. The pressure of her grinding on my cock makes my balls heavy, and I have to thank past me for getting those condoms, because if we were bare, Claire's thighs clenching as she rides me, her swollen lips parted with every pant and gasp, her nipples hard and firm, I'd be fuckin' done for.

She rides me for what seems like forever, writhing against my cock, tossing her head back, her hair growing damp with sweat and my fingers going numb from twisting and tweaking her nips.

She tenses, and she cries out so loud I bet the entire fucking compound hears her, but I don't care. Claire comes apart for me, crying my name, and trembling as I find my own release. Finally, she stills and collapses against my chest. She falls hard with almost her full weight, and I laugh, wrapping my arms around her and holding her while she cools.

I plant kisses against the top of her head and hold

her tight until I think she falls asleep, her fingers stroking the muscles of my pecs.

My dick is going soft inside her when she murmurs against my bare chest, "Can you fuck me from behind?"

Fuck yes, I can!

"You sure?" I ask.

Her eyes fly open, and she scratches her nails lightly against my skin. "Savage, don't you want to keep fucking me?"

"Say no more."

She lifts her face to me, and I kiss her, then we flip around until she's lying facedown, her head turned to the side. She lifts her ass, and my mouth waters. I lower my face to the smooth cheeks and grip them between my fingers.

"Fuck, this ass." I bite her cheek softly, not hard enough to leave a mark, and she widens her legs and moans in response.

"It's all yours, babe," she promises. "I'm all yours."

I kneel between her legs and urge her to lift up so she's kneeling, her head still resting forward on the bed. I can see her swollen pussy, wet with her juices, and as badly as I want to lean down and taste her, I do not want to come anywhere but deep inside her.

I watch, my fingers anchored on her hips, as every inch of my cock slides deep inside her. The moan she releases into the bedding as I thrust in takes my breath away. She wiggles her ass, writhing to get closer to me to bring me deeper, and I vow to oblige.

I pull all the way out and slam back into her, and the

steady rhythm of my thrusts and the slapping sound of my body banging into her has her crying again, "More, Savage, my God."

She begs and shoves her hips back, and I work her body until my knees go numb, sliding into her wetness and back out with such ease, it's as if her body was built for me. I pick up speed, squeezing her hips so hard, I'm afraid I'm leaving marks—which I absolutely don't want to do, but she's begging for more, and pretty soon, my rational thought is gone.

All I feel is her body, the heat of us mingling as sweat and movement, breath and need, until finally, lightning strikes, and I release into the condom, fully seated inside Claire.

When I'm done, it's my turn to flip onto the bed, boneless, sweaty, and more satisfied than I can ever remember being. I bring her close to my chest, wrap her in my arms, and fall asleep before I even take off the condom.

I wake at some point a few minutes later, or maybe it's a few hours, and I peel off the condom. My movement wakes Claire, and she takes the condom from me and then wipes off my dick with her fingers, which wakes him right back up again.

"Can you fuck me again?" she asks.

Through the dark, I point to a fresh condom, and she grabs it and tears it open, and then, lying on our sides, Claire spooned against my front, I hook a hand under her knee and fuck her from behind until she's reaching between her legs to massage her clit. She's quieter the second time she comes, and I'm so exhausted, so drained, I let go with her, her pulsing walls squeezing me until I'm coming again right after her.

I pull out, take off the condom, and crash out, my face buried deep in Claire's hair, my arm over her body, and her bare ass pressed against my cock. Bliss. Peace. And maybe, just maybe, this is love. I fall asleep without giving the words a chance to form, though, and before I know it, I'm out.

I slide out of bed early the next morning while Claire is still asleep. I have shit to do today, and I can't do it while Claire's naked body is pressed against me.

I kiss her on the hair, and she reaches for my hand. "Are you going? Aurora's asleep in your room. Let me get her."

I smooth the tangles from her face. "I'll wear the clothes I had on last night. I'll change later. I gotta run some errands."

With one final kiss on her head, I slip out of the bedroom. I shower in Claire's bathroom then put back on the clothes I wore last night. The compound is quiet, except there is a light on in Phantom's office and the door is cracked open. He's on the phone, speaking in low tones, and I wonder if he was here all night.

It's rare now for Phantom to sleep at the compound. He's got his teenage daughters, Poppy's son, and their baby on the way back at his house on the canal. But sometimes, the shit we do here is a full-time job.

I grab the keys to my bike and head out to the lot. I have sunglasses and a bandana stashed in the bike, so I suit up, but I don't wear my leathers. Today is a day job for me, for my shit.

I drive where the road takes me for a while before finding myself in the place I thought I'd never go. The parking lot of Pancake Circus is pretty empty at this hour. A few older folks sit together at tables, and some young people sit in booths working over laptops and bottomless cups of coffee.

I turn off the bike but leave my sunglasses on as I peer through the windows. I debate whether I should go in. It's the same fight I've had with myself every day for years. I know she's in there. I know her schedule almost down to the hour.

Her thick white hair calls to me like a beacon. I scrape the heels of my heavy boots against the asphalt, debating. I don't even have to say anything. I could go in, get a cup of coffee, and leave.

My heart bangs against the cage of my chest like a terrified rabbit. What the hell am I doing here? What is it about Claire that makes me want to face shit? Look the past in the eye and set things right?

I shake my head as I shove the memories away.

Why am I here?

What could I possibly hope to accomplish by being here? Forgiveness?

A fresh start?

There's no such thing for a man like me.

What Claire is doing is different. She has a baby to be strong for. She has a future to build.

My future is locked in a toxic choke hold with the past. I'm not working toward anything. There's nothing here for me.

I curse myself—and the weakness that brings me back here every week.

I fire up my bike and speed out of the lot, and I don't let myself think until I'm in a small driveway. I pull my bike into my assigned spot, then head upstairs to a second-floor unit. I unlock the door and let myself in for the first time since I met Claire.

I have a condo about three miles from the compound. It's not much. Two bedrooms, one bath. Since I stay in my room with the Heat most of the time, while Claire's getting herself on her feet, I want her to have more than a compound bedroom, the gravel driveway for Aurora to play on, and a shared space with a couple dozen bikers and bitches to call home.

Not to mention that the prospects are hankering for a party, and there's no bigger cockblock to a club party than a woman and a baby.

I want her someplace better. The best I can give her right now isn't much, but it's more than the shitty double bed she's been sleeping on.

I look around the place. It's dusty, but everything

works. There is a common space in the back and a small front yard with a manicured lawn. My unit has a spacious balcony, and I measure the privacy slats to make sure they are narrow enough to keep Aurora safe. I have no stairs in my place, and the floor plan is open.

I drop down onto the couch and survey the condo and what I'm about to do. My brain wants to run through all the scenarios. All the reasons I should not do this.

I pace the floors, wrestling with the possibilities and the massive decision ahead of me. But then I think of her, of my mother. I close my eyes and think if she'd had one person who could have offered her a real way out, maybe she could have taken me and left. Maybe she wouldn't have lost teeth and self-respect, her sanity and me.

It doesn't matter what happens in the future. I decide I'll deal with it when I need to. I may not be able to give Claire me, but I can give her this. More than I could do for my mother. More than anyone could do for her. I can give her a chance to start over, and that's the least she deserves.

TWELVE
CLAIRE

THE LAST WEEK has flown by. I still go to the diner early in the morning to get some work done, and then Aurora and I spend the afternoons and evenings setting up Savage's condo.

Tank and a couple of the other guys have moved over the crib and all the things Aurora has been using at the compound. Savage's place has a bathtub with a shower in it, so I'm going to be able to give Aurora real baths.

Savage has a small table and chairs in the kitchen, which I'll use as a desk when I look for jobs.

Today is my last day at the compound. I'm planning on sleeping at Savage's condo tonight. And I hope he might consider staying there with me. I have a little something special planned for him. A surprise that I hope shows him how much I appreciate everything he's doing for me.

Val refills my coffee and bends to chat with Aurora. "How were those pancakes, honeybun?"

"Mama." Aurora slaps her hands against the table, her mood a lot better than it was last week. She did cut a new tooth, and she's been sleeping better, thank goodness.

"Well, that sounds good to me." Val laughs. "Can I get either one of you anything else?"

I nod and prepare to put my plan in motion. "So, do you know if the diner makes deliveries? I was hoping to have a special dinner for a friend tonight, and I wanted to maybe have dinner delivered to my new place."

"Oh, congratulations." Val gathers up my empty plate. "We do have one of those phone app delivery services. We close down to orders, though, if we're really busy in the dining room. So, maybe order in advance?"

That's what I was afraid of. "I don't have a credit card right now," I tell her. "I was hoping to pay cash for the meal and the delivery." I've been working my way through the money Savage has given me, but I still don't have a bank account or a credit card of my own. I imagine it will be a long time before I have any of that.

She nods. "I understand that. Where is your place, hun, and what time do you need the food?"

I give her the address of the condo, and she looks a little surprised. "That's only about three miles from my place. It's on my way home."

My heart suddenly lurches into overdrive. I turn to Val. "My friend is Savage, the guy who orders out all the time. I think he'd lose his mind if you delivered our dinner tonight. His favorite waitress."

Her eyes widen. "Is Savage your boyfriend, honey? I didn't know that."

I cock my head. "It's complicated." I reach out and touch little Aurora's hand. "I have a baby and just got out of a bad situation. He's got some history of his own, and for now, we're friends."

"Close friends, I hope." Val gives me a smile and then leans in. She tears a piece of paper off her notepad. "Write your order and your address here, honey. And if you don't mind, give me a cell phone number. That way, if anything goes wrong, I can reach out. Just don't tell my boss I made a delivery for you. I don't think that's covered under their insurance, and he's a bit of a stickler for the rules." She looks at me and Aurora and smiles. "But for my cutest customers, we can bend those rules a bit."

"How do I pay you?" I ask. "I can leave a large tip now, and you can pay for the dinner…"

She waves a hand at me. "You can reimburse me when I get there. No problem, honey." She points to the table. "Just leave the order and your info on the table." She winks at me. "I'm excited. I'm in on a happy little surprise."

I smile at her and realize I'm excited too. I know this isn't my money, but I have been so dependent on Savage. He was planning on dropping me off at his condo and turning over the keys tonight, so having a little something to thank him has been on my mind all week. His favorite diner dinner isn't much, but it's something I hope lets him know how much I appreciate everything he's doing for me.

After I gather up Aurora and my laptop, Tank pulls into the lot to pick me up. "Change of plans," he announces. "You up for a pit stop?"

I shrug. "Sure," I say. We have no real schedule to keep today. "Where to?"

Tank meets my eyes in the mirror. "Ask Poppy. This is all her idea."

I have no idea what Poppy has in store, but I buckle in and watch the road roll by as Tank takes me to a part of town I've never been to. We pull into a small but very pretty strip mall.

"Out ya go." He jerks a thumb toward the mall. "I'll wait here. I'm gonna text my gal and see if she's up for a party tonight."

I laugh. The compound's probably planning the party to end all parties after almost months of having a mama and baby underfoot. "Well, I hope she's able to make it."

I like Tank, and I'm a little sad that I might not see him every day anymore. I won't have a car at Savage's, and he told me he'll make sure I have rides whenever I need them, but it will be different once I'm no longer under the Heat's roof. No more walking out and seeing what Tank's up to, if he has the time to run me someplace.

He air-fives Aurora, who is now a pro at high fives, but she laughs harder when Tank intentionally misses.

"Uncle Tank," he says, enunciating every syllable, hoping that she'll start to say it.

She blows a very wet raspberry and laughs, and Tank shakes his head. "Close, kid. You're getting close."

I wave at him and head through the parking lot to where I see Poppy standing in front of one of the shops. She's waving excitedly and rocking up and down on her heels.

"Claire." When I get close enough, she opens her arms. I set the detachable part of Aurora's car seat down on the concrete so I can give Poppy a full-body hug. "Hi, friend. How are you?"

I smile, her beauty and poise no longer a source of shame. I may have very little, but I'm clean. I'm trying. That's all that matters.

"I'm great," I tell her. "But what's going on?" I check the time on my burner phone. I'm supposed to meet Savage back at the compound around six.

"So..." Poppy smiles. "I hear today is a big day for you, and I wanted to start things off in style. Give you a little moving-home present just from me."

I shake my head, confused. "You've done so much. What on earth do you want to do now?"

She holds the door open and motions me to go ahead of her. As soon as I get inside, Holly and Daisy, Poppy's stepdaughters, jump up from the gorgeous leather couch in the waiting area.

"Aurora." They shriek in unison and run toward me. "Hi, Claire. Hi, Claire." Their voices carry over each other, and I laugh.

They've come to the compound to visit their dad and play with Aurora just a couple of times, but they are really sweet, loving girls. They take turns giving me huge hugs, like I'm a long-lost aunt they are absolutely thrilled to finally see again. At first, the affection feels overwhelming, but when I see Poppy's encouraging smile, I accept their hugs and relax a bit.

These are genuine people. I was a good person once. And I'm slowly, slowly crawling my way back. Someday, I'll be able to repay every one of these people for their kindness. For now, I feed on it, sucking it in gratefully and doing what I can to give it back.

"You two are the sweetest," I say, looking from older sister to younger. They are so different from each other —Holly, the older, more sensitive and reserved one, and Daisy, all sass and colorful hair. She's got a vibrant strip of blue in her hair, and I motion toward it.

"Is that fresh?" I ask. "You look amazing." I turn to Holly. "And I hate to say it, but if I'd known you in high school, I would have been so jealous." I touch the soft ends of Holly's hair, curled in perfect, beachy waves. "You're like teen models."

They laugh and shake their heads, too excited about whatever they have planned for compliments. Daisy shows me a huge backpack.

"So, Ma said we could bring a few things."

"A few," Holly teases. "And then of course Daisy wanted everything."

"Shut up," Daisy snaps, but then she makes eye

contact with her mom and says, "I mean, come on, Hol. We needed all this."

They pull out an assortment of toys and books, as well as a small blanket that they unfold and spread out on the pristine floor of the empty waiting area.

"What is this?" I ask.

Poppy claps her hands. "Spa day. I'm going to give you a fresh look while the kids take care of Aurora." She points to a chair not far from the waiting room. "My station is right there, so you'll be able to see them the whole time."

I shake my head. I can't accept this.

I feel the ends of my hair. I've been trimming my own hair with scissors for over two years. It's long, like waist-length, but I keep it as healthy as I can under the circumstances. I wouldn't even know what to ask for.

"Poppy, this is your business. I can't—"

"My treat," Poppy says. "It's a housewarming gift. And besides, I'm going to be going on maternity leave soon, so I wanted to give you something a little special before I'm off duty for a few months."

"Okay," I whisper, not wanting to be rude.

I leave Aurora with Daisy and Holly, and I can't help but feel impressed and relieved at the same time.

If I end up getting a job again, childcare is going to be a very real concern. For now, Aurora getting used to new people, more than just me, is a process for me too. I'm grateful to have these safe and small steps to move us both forward through the past.

Poppy starts me off with a consult, and we talk about hairstyles and length.

"Hear me out," she says. She takes a small amount of hair from the front and bends it over my forehead. "Have you ever had bangs? I am seeing a gorgeous wispy fringe to set off those gorgeous green eyes."

My eyes sting with tears as I picture my mom. Dawn always had long, wispy bangs. It was a hairstyle that I associated with her and truly could never see on myself. But in Poppy's chair, her soft scent filling my nose, the happy sounds of music and chatter echoing through the salon, I find myself unexpectedly open to anything.

I close my eyes and nod. "I'm gonna trust you. Style, length, whatever. I trust you."

Poppy sends me off to the shampoo bowl, where a girl named Anna gives me the head massage of my life. I'm practically sound asleep when the water turns on, and she gets me all rinsed and ready for my cut. After the wash, Poppy is still finishing with a customer, so she sends Anna back to dry me, and then another girl comes to give me a mini-manicure—just a nail soak, file, and cuticle trim—at the chair. I've got one girl working on my hands and Anna drying my hair, and for the first time, I let myself feel hopeful.

My life was like this once. Haircuts and spa days. Manicures, pedicures, and pretty clothes. I can be that way again. I can become the person I know I am meant to be. I lost my way for a short time, but I've learned. I'm stronger now. I have a daughter and a purpose. I let hope wash over me like the hot air from the dryer as Anna gets me ready.

By the time Poppy comes over to dry-cut me, my shoulders are relaxed and I'm ready for a nap. We chatter while she trims my length, taking a couple of inches off. She adds soft layers and asks me about what I plan to do once I'm all settled in the condo.

"I need a job," I tell her. I tell her about my old job as a paralegal, and we chat about whether I would go back into the same field. "To be honest," I tell her, "I'd like to do something else. I didn't love the work when I had it, but I was happy to get a good job that paid well and had advancement. After two years out of the workforce, I'll take anything."

She nods. "I'll have to ask my mom."

"Ask Mom what?" Another woman sidles up to the chair and stands behind Poppy in the mirror. I can see the resemblance.

"Oh, this is perfect. Claire," she says to me, "I'd like you to meet my sister. Her name is Clara."

"Is this the famous Claire I've been hearing so much about?" Poppy's sister sets a hand on my shoulder and gives me a squeeze through the plastic salon smock. "I've been telling Poppy to get you in here."

"Nice to meet you," I say.

While Poppy and her sister talk about their mother, I can't help but marvel at the coincidence. I wonder what it would be like to have a sister? Someone to lean on instead of being alone. Besides my mother and now

Aurora, I've never seen my facial features on anyone else. It would be a trip, for sure.

"Would you be open to that, Claire?" Poppy asks.

I look up and meet her eyes in the mirror. I was so lost in my own thoughts, I don't know what she said. "Sorry. Would I be open to what?" I ask.

Poppy smiles. "My mom works in local government. I'll ask if she knows anybody who's hiring. She knows so many people in this town, you never know."

I physically turn and look at Poppy, my mouth wide open. "You would do that? You would ask your mom to help me find a job?"

"Don't get your hopes up," Clara says. "Mom can be really tough on people. She'll want to meet you and vet you…and probably ask for a DNA sample."

Poppy smacks her sister on the arm. "Mom's not that bad." She leans forward and giggles. "If you could imagine what it was like introducing Mom to Phantom." She puts a hand over her heart. "Trust me. Mom will see what we all see in you, and she'll bend over backward to help."

I'm struck silent as they chat while Poppy finishes off my hair. I don't even know how to process this level of kindness. I think back to what Stella said those first few days I was in the compound. How everyone there is here for a reason. I wonder about Stella, Tank, Phantom, and Shadow. All the people who welcomed me in have stories of their own.

I have to imagine a woman who falls in love with a man like that was drawn to him for a reason. Yes, he's quiet and has two incredible daughters, but I'm seeing for the first time that maybe I really am one of them. One of those people. I just happen to be at the start of my story, not the end.

By the time I look back up in the mirror, Poppy is smoothing down my hair with a beautiful hair balm that makes the new length bounce and all of it feel silky soft. I look at myself, and I can't stop the grin that flies across my face. I see my mom's long, fringed bangs but on my face. And Poppy was right. I look fantastic. Like a completely different woman.

I jump up from the chair and pull Poppy into a hug. "I love it," I tell her. "For so long, I've looked in the mirror and seen someone who I couldn't believe was me." I think back to the black eye I had when Poppy met me. By the look on her face, I know she's thinking about it too. "This is the most me I think I've ever felt in my life. Thank you. Thank you so, so much."

She rocks me back and forth and sniffles, no doubt fighting the same tears that I am. "You're welcome," she says. "Just always believe that this is you. That the you that you want to be is never far away. Sometimes you just have to look hard for her."

We release each other, and I notice Tank hovering in the front entryway. He nods at Holly and Daisy, but his eyes are locked on the shampoo girl, Anna. Poppy takes off my smock, and I thank the girls for watching Aurora. I can tell Aurora's ready for a nap, and I'm thankful for it or I suspect she'd throw a tantrum at my taking her away from her new best friends. The girls gather up the toys while I put Aurora back in her car seat.

"Can I tip the shampoo girl, at least?" I ask Poppy. I think it would be weird to tip Poppy when she said the services were her treat, but Anna gave me both a stellar head massage and an absolutely brilliant shampoo.

"Okay," Poppy says thoughtfully. "You don't have to, though. I'll take care of her."

"No," I say. "Savage gave me some cash. I'd like to."

I consider walking over to where she's standing at the front counter looking over an iPad, but then I get another idea. I walk up to Tank, Aurora's car carrier in my hands. "How'd it go with your lady friend?" I ask. "You got a date for the big party tonight?"

Tank grunts and shoves his hands into his pockets. "Totally friend-zoned," he says sadly.

I put a hand on his arm. "I'm sorry, Tank. Her loss. You know that, right?"

He shrugs and holds the door open for me. I head out, but once we're partway to the truck, I stop and pretend I forgot to tip the shampoo girl. "Oh no," I say, putting a sad look on my face. "Tank, can you do me a huge favor?"

"Sure, doll."

I point back at the shop and hold out my hand with a ten-dollar bill in it. "The shampoo girl, Anna. Could you run this into her? I forgot to tip her, but I want to get Aurora into the truck. If we go back in and she sees Holly and Daisy, I think she's gonna start fussing."

Tank nods and takes the money, but then I see him

shuffle on his boots and blush as he hands Anna the tip. They talk for a few minutes before he finally heads back to the truck. I pretend I didn't see the whole thing and act like I just finished buckling Aurora in when he climbs behind the wheel.

"Sorry to ask you to do that," I say. "But I appreciate it."

He is still beet red, and he has a small smile on his face. "Not a problem," he says, then heads the truck back toward the compound.

Tank's a good kid. Poppy's an amazing friend. Savage is a great buddy, I guess. Whatever I have and however long it lasts, I'm thrilled that I could pay even the smallest amount forward.

A few hours later, I take one last look around my room. Everything has been packed up except one final small load that we'll move to the condo.

My heart thuds in my chest, and I sit on the floor with Aurora for the last time. There's a knock on my door, and I call out, "Come on in." I haven't locked the door in weeks. The key sits unused on one of the bedside tables.

I'm surprised when it's Phantom who sticks his head in and nods at me.

"Phantom," I stand up, leaving Aurora playing on the floor. I look at the massive man in front of me and don't know what to say. This is goodbye, and I wouldn't have expected him to stop by to see me. But since he has, I feel like this is the universe giving me permission to say everything that's been on my mind. "I will never, ever be able to repay you."

He holds up a hand, but I take it in mine. He looks at me, shocked. I squeeze his hand in mine, then release it, tears in my eyes. "Poppy," I say, tears streaming down my face. "And you, Holly, and Daisy."

I suddenly don't have the words I thought I did. I glance up at his gruff face, and he looks a little lost. "Everything okay?" he asks quietly.

I do the only thing that I can. I have no flowery speech telling him how much their kindness, his generosity, has meant to me. These people saved my life. I don't know where I'd be or how I'd be if they hadn't taken me in. Even if Savage had bought my freedom, it was a completely different thing for these bikers and their families to take me under their wing.

I throw myself against Phantom's chest and wrap my arms around him. "Thank you," I say, my heart in my throat. "Thank you."

He awkwardly pats my back.

I step back and wipe the tears from my eyes. If I'm not mistaken, I see a glimmer in his dark eyes too.

He just nods and barks, "All right." Then he turns to leave, but he suddenly turns back. "Door's always open," he says, but then he flicks a look at Aurora, releases a full-face smile, and leaves.

I drop back down on the floor and stroke Aurora's hair. "That didn't go the way I'd planned," I laugh. But with luck, the rest of the night will be just perfect. I got a text from Val a few minutes ago confirming the time she will stop by with dinner. Now all I need is for Savage to come get me, and this chapter of my life will close.

When Savage arrives, he's dressed in black jeans and a black button-down shirt. He's wearing his broken-in motorcycle boots, and he looks so gorgeous, dressed more for a date than for moving somebody in to their new place.

I grin at him.

His mouth drops open. "What did you do?" he asks.

I touch a hand to my hair, for a moment panicked that he doesn't like it. "My haircut?" I rush out. "Poppy, she offered to give me a…"

But the words die on my lips when Savage strides over to me and touches the lengths that fall over my shoulders like he's touching glass. "You look stunning," he murmurs. "I thought you were beautiful before, but…" He swallows and widens his eyes. "My God, Claire."

I throw myself at him, but this is a very different hug from the one I gave Phantom. I crush myself against him and lift my lips to his face. Our kisses are slow and deep, and they are over way too quickly.

"Let's get you out of here." His face is flushed, his breaths coming in as fast as mine. If things go well, maybe we can pick up where we left off later. He looks down at Aurora, composing his face into a smile. "You ready to go to your own home, little lady?"

Aurora does something then that nearly sends me to my knees. She holds her arms up to Savage. Not to me. To Savage.

He freezes and looks at me. "What should I do?"

I smile, my heart breaking into a million happy pieces. "She wants you to pick her up," I say. "But I can do it if you're not comfortable."

"Are you?" he asks. "It's okay?"

I shake my head, as if to dismiss the ridiculous thought. "Of course." What I don't say is that I trust him. It's been slow coming, but I do. I trust him with my baby, and with me… Maybe not fully, but for now, it's more than enough.

THIRTEEN
SAVAGE

WHEN I PICK up Aurora and start carrying her through the compound, let's just say Claire and I attract some stares.

"Claire!" Stella's full-volume shout stops us both in our tracks.

Blade, our club treasurer, is sitting at the bar making googly eyes at Stella while she sips something out of a mega cup covered in sparkles.

She comes bouncing around the bar, waddles up to us on huge heels, and squeals. "A new home, a fresh start." She pulls Claire into a hug and looks her deep in the eyes. "Don't be a stranger. You have my number. You need anything." She flicks a look at me holding Aurora. "Except babysitting. When she's old enough for makeup and boys, I'm your gal. But anything else—" she kisses Claire loudly on the cheek "—you call."

Claire nods and rocks Stella back and forth in a hard

hug. "Thank you," she breathes against Stella's heavily sprayed hair.

I get stares from some of my brothers, including Blade, but Viper comes up to us as we're nearing the door. He looks me over and shakes his head, but then he claps a hand on my shoulder.

"See you later?" he asks.

I'm not sure what he means by that, so I don't say much. Viper ain't one for kids and families, so I'm sure he assumes that after Phantom and Shadow, I'll be the next to fall.

"Catch you later," I say, but I don't say any more. I'll be back. I just don't know yet when that will be.

Shadow comes in the door just as we're heading out. "Hey, glad I caught you." He holds out a gift bag that's purple and overstuffed with shit. "Books," he explains, holding it out to Claire. "Mostly for Aurora. Violet sent these as a little housewarming gift."

Claire looks at the bag and then at Shadow, and she steps up to the man, rising on her toes to kiss his cheek. "Please tell her thank you." She shakes her head. "You've all done so much. Thank you, Shadow."

Shadow looks at me, then narrows his eyes. He waves off Claire's thanks with a hand. "I'll be seeing you," he says, then stumbles past me, giving me one more long look.

I don't care how it looks, me carrying Claire's kid. She's got her arms full, and fuck, the baby wanted *me*. But it doesn't mean anything. It sure doesn't mean anything to me—at least, that's what I tell myself.

We head over to my pickup truck, where Tank's moving the car seat into the back seat. After he's done, he comes up to me and takes little Aurora's arm in his and slightly slaps her hand against his palm. "High five, baby doll."

Aurora laughs hysterically, a belly-jiggling, dimple-making laugh, and Claire gives Tank a hug.

"You call me anytime," he says. "This guy's paying for my gas, so I'll take you wherever you need to go."

"All right, fuck off with the long goodbyes," I growl, but I can't help feeling warm inside.

Claire's made an impression around here—and not just on me. She's quiet but has come into her own. She's healed and changed in the time she's been with us, and I'm feeling grateful as fuck for the family I have that stood behind her while she was at her lowest. It's what this brotherhood is supposed to be. It's who we are.

We're trouble and we're not exactly squeaky-clean, but we're a family.

The words stick in my throat, but I'm even more shocked when Claire climbs into the passenger seat beside me.

"She'll be okay alone?" I ask, widening my eyes and looking back at Aurora.

"Yeah," Claire assures me. "It's a short ride. I gave her some toys. She'll be fine."

When she straps herself in and looks at me out of the corner of her eye, I can't stop feeling like this is my family too. This woman, with her gorgeous new haircut, those bangs that make her eyes look even prettier, the way she crosses her legs in the passenger seat. It's like we're on a date, and I have to grip the wheel with both hands to stop myself from reaching for her.

This is a move for Claire's good. So she can get her head on straight and find a job and settle into a routine with her daughter that doesn't include playing on the floor of a motorcycle club compound.

This is not about Claire and me.

But as I park the truck in front of my condo, it's hard not to feel it. I was never a guy who dreamed about my future. I've always looked over my shoulder, watched for the demons that chased me every step of every day. But now, I look at Claire beside me, the condo ahead, and the only thing I see behind me is a perfect baby with crystal-blue eyes and a dimpled smile that can break down your walls.

I shake my head and turn off the engine. "Welcome home," I say, the double meaning of my words making my voice thick.

Claire hugs her arms around herself and takes a deep breath. "Welcome home to you too. This will always be your home, even if it's cluttered with a lot more clothes, toys, and dirty diapers."

"Speaking of," I say, "when do kids start using the toilet?"

Claire laughs and shakes her head. "It's gonna be a while," she says.

Then she turns in her seat and looks at Aurora. "Baby, you ready?"

"Mama."

I let myself out of the truck and grab the last of Claire's bags. She unbuckles the baby seat and brings Aurora in the carrier, while I grab the base so she can put it in any car she needs it in the next time she gets a ride someplace.

Every step up to the front door feels huge, like I'm walking into a wild, uncertain future. I'm nervous. I won't lie. I promised to protect her, and now she'll be under her own roof. And the idea that she's not just down the hall anymore sends my guts into a tailspin.

I have to shake it off, though, so I hand her the keys and watch as she unlocks the door. She shoves the door open and walks in, then looks back to see why I'm not following.

I give her a grin. "Can I come in?"

She plays along, shaking her head as if she's thinking about it. "Hm, I don't normally let strange men into my place, but I'll make an exception." She lowers her voice and pretends to cover one of Aurora's ears. "Because you have such a nice ass."

I laugh and follow her in, and I lock the door behind me. We spend about half an hour setting up the last of her things.

"Can you stay a while?" she asks after the books from Shadow and Violet have been put away. "I have a little tiny surprise for you."

Something in her voice sends a shiver up the back of my spine and then down to my dick. Claire goes off to the kitchen to make dinner for Aurora, and I follow her, carrying Aurora on one hip.

"I don't like surprises," I tell her.

It's the truth. But just like the day I met her—which was a huge fucking surprise, by the way—maybe I should be a little more open to the unexpected. I lean down and kiss her bare shoulder. "But maybe just this once."

She rolls her head back toward me, and I kiss the top of her hair. Her hair smells so damned delicious, it makes my mouth water. I want to kiss her, hold her, and yet, I have to hold back. I'm giving her this place, and she needs to turn a page. Find herself and her future.

I assume that future is gonna go in a very different direction than the path I'm on.

The less messy I can make this for myself and my heart, the better.

I'm bouncing Aurora on my hip when there is a firm knock at the door. Claire turns and faces me, a wide grin on her beautiful face. I take a moment to just look at her. Really look at her. Gone are the bruises and the matted hair. The filthy clothes and the fear.

The woman before me is a vision. Someone I think—no, I know—I could learn to love. If I were the kind of man who could ever love someone.

Claire bounces past me on her bare feet to answer the door, while I grab a piece of sliced banana and hand it to Aurora.

"Looks good, kid," I tell her. "You wanna share?"

I open my mouth, but Aurora stuffs her fingers into her mouth and chomps loudly on a banana.

"Gotta respect the appetite," I say, nodding.

Something catches my ear, though, as I hear Claire chatting up someone in the entryway. A sudden flare of worry crests through my gut, and a protective instinct, soul-deep and pounding against the back of my ribs like a drumbeat, has me holding tighter to Aurora as I walk to the front door.

What greets me immediately are two things that my shocked brain processes at the same time. The smell of diner food and a very familiar voice. It comes to me through water, over years and miles and memories. I can only hear her part of the conversation, but I can hardly make out what she's saying over the ringing in my ears.

"Savage is here right now," Claire is saying. *"No, that's not Savage. That kid's name is Tank. I know, it's cute, right? He's a sweetheart. You've never met him? Why don't you come in and meet him?"*

Claire turns to me, and everything suddenly shifts into slow motion. Val from the diner walks through Claire's front door. I see her white hair first, the cut so familiar after all these years. She's wearing real clothes, not her diner uniform. She looks thicker, which is good. She's put on some weight. She's wearing blue jeans and a light blue sweater, a pair of glasses hanging around her neck from a chain.

She takes one look at my face, the baby in my arms,

and then my face again. She freezes. "Ethan?" she asks, her hands flying to her mouth.

Claire cocks her chin and looks confused. Her eyes shift from Val to me. I see recognition cross her face. She knows my real name is Ethan, and yet it's clear she has no idea how Val knows that.

I swallow hard and make an impossible choice in the span of under a second. First, I lower my face to Aurora's little head and kiss her lightly. Her baby hair is so soft, I almost change my mind. Is there nothing we wouldn't do for our kids? For our parents? I can't, though. I fucking can't.

I walk over to Claire, pass her Aurora, and say, "I can't fucking do this. I'm sorry, Claire. I'm sorry, Mom."

Then I walk past Val, shove the door open, and run full speed to my truck.

I'm three beers in before anybody dares to talk to me. Phantom sits down next to me but doesn't say anything. Music blares from speakers set all over the compound, and since it's the first night anybody's really partied in months, the vibe is upbeat and maybe a little too rowdy.

I don't belong anywhere. Not with my brothers jamming on video-game controllers. Not with my head thrown back in a recliner, some hot, skinny body anchored to my lap. Not here. Not anywhere. I stormed in after leaving Claire's, jammed my keys in my pocket, and demanded a beer from Stella, who looked like she had a lot of questions. But reading the look on my face, she popped the top off a bottle and left me to my sulking.

Phantom claps a hand on my shoulder and squeezes. Then he walks away into the crowd. That shoulder-clap was an invitation, reassurance, a whole lot all in one movement, but I don't want it.

I just need not to think and not to feel.

I finish off my third beer, and my eyes sear over the crowd. Everyone is letting loose, having a good time, and just like always, I'm the odd man out. In pain when I should be walking on top of the world. At the height of my career, respected, stable, when what I really am is a fucking fist who rides a bike. I make my money any way I can. My values are in the toilet. Honor is a thing I used to think I knew, but now, I don't feel as if even my brotherhood can save me.

I don't know what I was trying to do, saving a broken woman when I can't even save myself.

I've thought about how it happened a thousand ways to Sunday since I stormed out of the condo. And it's all my own goddamned fault. If I'd never introduced Claire to the diner, if I'd never let the parts of my world cross like this, Claire would never have thought to surprise me with my favorite dinner.

I don't know how she got Val to drop off the meal, but it was obvious from the look on her face that she had no idea I'd be there. She had no idea I was Savage, which relieves me even more.

But now, even that is ruined. The one good thing I could do to make up the past to my ma is now fucked too.

This is why I fucking hate surprises.

I abandon my empty bottle on the bar and am about to leave when Stella's soft voice says, "You look like you need more than another drink."

I shake my head, discouraging any more questions, and push up from the barstool.

"Savage, wait." She leans over the bar toward me, giving me an eyeful of cleavage.

I look away. It somehow feels disrespectful to Claire to even look. But then I force myself to glance back.

Claire is nothing to me. She's not mine. I can look at whomever and whatever I want.

I meet Stella's eyes, and the genuine concern in them makes me regret doing it.

"What?" I grit out, my voice rough and angry. "Just say what you gotta say, Stel."

She stands upright and crosses her arms over her chest. "I will, then. And if you still want to be a prick to the people who care about you, be my guest." She leans back on the bar and points a finger in my face. Her fake nail is like a laser pointer aiming for my head. "I don't know your shit, man, but that girl—that woman and that baby—are special. You saw something in them. That's why you did what you did and got them out of a bad situation."

"That's bullshit," I tell her. "I didn't see shit. I did what any human being would do." I run a hand through my hair and tug hard on the ends. "And that shit got out of hand."

"Why?" she demands, her voice harsh in its honesty. "Because you gave up money, your room, your fucking condo for that woman? Why did you do that, Savage? Because she's some charity case you picked up on the street?" She shakes her head, her stiffly sprayed hair barely moving. "You did what you did because there's something real there. You care about her, Savage."

I shake my head. "I don't."

She waves a hand at me, dismissing me. "Tell yourself whatever you want. I don't care. But I also know that you're a man who has a code. You're different from the rest of these guys, and no, it's not because you were in the military. A bunch of these shitheads were."

She looks at me so hard, I swear she can see through me. I flinch on instinct, hoping she really can't. I don't want anyone to see it all.

"Whatever you went through, whatever trauma or guilt or even just bad fucking memories that woman brought up for you, it doesn't fucking matter, Savage. The past only controls you if you let it. Look at Claire, what she's been through. In the time she was here, she learned to trust. I'd have thought you'd have learned the same thing." She reaches across the bar and cups my chin. "We all carry it, Savage. Whatever you think you're carrying, you're not the only one. And it doesn't make you broken. It makes you one of us."

"Good talk, Stel." Her words make sense. Every

single thing coming out of her mouth is real and feels right. It just doesn't fix anything. It doesn't fix me.

I get up and turn to leave but not before I see her give me the middle finger. "Savage," she seethes. I can tell she's actually angry now. "I don't give a shit about kids, you know that, right?"

I look over my shoulder at her and shrug. I'm ready for this conversation to be over.

"Aurora trusts you. That should tell you more than whatever the voices in your head are saying." With that, she makes another vulgar gesture at me, but then she looks at me gently, with pity. Which is exactly what I don't want or need.

I storm down the hallway to my room and slam the door as hard as I fucking can. It does nothing to relieve the pent-up anger and confusion. I pace the floor, the heels of my boots scuffing marks into the vinyl flooring. Everywhere I look, I see signs of what should be here… who was here.

I can't be in this room. Don't want these reminders, and yet I am drawn to be even closer to them. I leave my room and head toward Claire's. As soon as I open the door, I can tell coming in here was a big mistake. The space still smells like her. The lavender baby lotion she rubs on Aurora before she goes to sleep.

The bed we slept in, talked in together for weeks, is neatly made, all traces of her, the long hair that spilled over those pillows, gone. There are no clothes in the closet, and even the crib is gone, now taking up space in a bedroom in my condo.

It's as if they disappeared from my reality forever.

Just like my parents when I left.

But I know they aren't here. They are out there somewhere, just like my mom and just like my old man.

I can't be with them. I can't be a part of whatever peaceful, sweet life they are making. I can't be a part of the dark side of love, because no matter what we do, it's always there. The broken parts inside us can't be healed. They can only be hidden or buried, suppressed for a time. And then when they are triggered, they come out swinging.

And that is exactly what I intend to do. I need to hurt something, and I need to do it tonight.

I grab a baseball bat that I keep under my bed. I don't want any guns, no weapons that can be traced back to the club. But I think back to the assholes who beat me down when we tried to collect what they owed us, and I know what I need to do.

I leave the compound through the front door, not saying goodbye to anyone. I ignore the heavy stares of Stella and Phantom and walk my way through the music and the laughter, the dancing and grinding, games and noise, like a robot programmed for one thing alone: destruction.

I fire up my truck and speed over to the other side of town. The entire drive, I can't calm down. I can't talk myself down from what I'm about to do. I don't think about the consequences. Just like that night with my dad. I'm enraged and on fire, and I don't know how to process what percolates inside me. I need to act, to hurt, to hit.

I'm gonna find the face of that punk-ass bitch who gave me a boot to the ribs, and I'm gonna start swinging.

I pull into a dark strip mall and park at the far end of the lot where I know the security cameras won't pick up my truck. When I'm here on legit business, I want the assholes who do business with us to know exactly who is here and why. But I don't want anything I do tonight to come back on the club.

I grab the baseball bat and picture the floor plan. There should be about twenty tables inside. It's still early, so the place won't be full yet. My mark usually rotates through the tables, playing where the cards are hot, so I'll have to do some looking before I find him. That means I have to carry the bat in with me.

I didn't fucking think this through. A single guy who looks like me carrying a baseball bat can't just walk into an illegal betting operation and not bring a hell of a lot of heat down on him. Maybe that's what I need. Maybe that's what I deserve.

I clench the bat in my hands and swing, my blood pressure rising until I feel like I need to smash something. I'm so riled up, I don't even hear the bike pulling up and parking next to my truck.

"Savage," an angry voice snaps.

I close my eyes. *Fuck.* "This has nothing to do with the Heat," I growl.

"The fuck it don't." Phantom's off his bike, walking

toward me at speeds I didn't know the massive man had in him.

He shakes his head at me. "Since when do you go off on a solo operation?"

"Since fucking when do you follow me, huh?" I clench the bat tighter and hold it up like I'm still thinking about swinging.

"Since you fucking storm out of the compound with a goddamn baseball bat in your hand." Phantom is a man of few words, but these land hard. He glares at me and shakes his head. "I don't know what the fuck is going on with you, but if you're trying to get yourself killed and bring a hell of a lot of pain down on us, you better have a goddamn good reason why."

I throw the bat down in fury and fist my hands. I land a punch on Phantom's jaw before I realize what I'm doing. The sensation breaks the frenzy I'm in. Phantom staggers back, holding his jaw with a hand and looking at me like he's ready to fucking murder me.

I hang my head and get ready to take it. "Do it," I tell him. "Fuckin' do it, man."

Phantom shakes his head at me, then bends down and picks up the baseball bat. That startles me, because I expected an eye for an eye. But this? The bat could kill me. Phantom might actually want to fucking kill me after I socked him in the face.

My mind works at warp speed while I watch Phantom adjust his hands on the grip of the bat.

I don't want to die.

I don't want to leave Claire.

I don't want to be hit.

I don't want to cry.

"I'm sorry, man!" I scream out, punching the air, punching out the fury, the pain. "I'm fucking sorry."

Phantom looks at the end of the bat, then at me. He lowers the bat so it's clear he's not going to hit me. Not yet, at least. Then he walks up to me and stabs a finger against my chest. "Get your fucking head right," he snaps. "You packin'?"

I shake my head. I intentionally didn't bring my guns.

"You lyin'?" he demands, narrowing his eyes at me.

"No," I say quietly.

Phantom nods. "I'm not gonna stand here and play daddy. Go fucking fix your shit. And don't come back until you're right with it."

He takes the bat and walks past me toward his bike, but as he passes me, he gives me another squeeze on the shoulder. "It's time, motherfucker," he says quietly. "Get right with yourself, for fuck's sake. For our sake, for Claire's sake." He says the name that he knows is buried deep behind all my emotions. "For your own damn sake."

He releases my shoulder, then winds up his arm, and tosses the baseball bat as far away as he can. I hear it tumble off into the scrub, consumed by the darkness that surrounds this shady location. Then he gets on his motorcycle and rides off.

I'm alone in the dark, my hands empty, my head so full it hurts.

I was made in violence.

I am violence.

It's what I fear, understand, and know.

And I hate it.

I hate the man who made me what I am.

I hate the love that cost me everything.

I even hate myself.

When another car pulls into the lot, I get into my truck and rest my head on the steering wheel. I've got nothing. No place to go. No way to get this rage out of my body.

And then I feel my phone vibrate with a text.

FOURTEEN
CLAIRE

I REREAD the text I sent to Savage for the billionth time since I sent it.

> Me: Val is gone. I'm so, so sorry. I would never do anything to hurt you. I didn't know. Please come home.

I don't know what parts of it will make him react, if any. But he hasn't responded, and it's been over an hour.

I'm terrified that he's not okay.

After Savage stormed out of here, I invited Val to stay. She wanted me to eat, but I had no appetite, so I put the dinners in the fridge, and we talked on the couch. While Aurora played at our feet, she told me the very short version of their story.

Arthur Everett, Savage's dad, was a brutal man. Violent when he wasn't drinking and cruel when he was.

"He didn't start out that way, of course," Val said, smoothing her hair down. "They never do. We met young, when we were in high school, and over the years, he changed. Anger and failure do things to people, and not everyone knows how to deal with it."

Val's voice was steady as she spoke, and she laced her fingers together as she stared down at them.

"My son tried to protect me, and I..." She shook her head. "I tried to stop him from having to. I really did. But I failed him. I failed my family and my son." She met my eyes. "He lost everything. His military career. His parents. There are no easy answers, and there is no one right thing to do in every situation. I believed that then, and I believe it now. I'm just sorry I didn't know how to protect my son and keep him in my life. He's never left my heart, though. And I have to wonder if I still have a place deep in his."

She laughed quietly. "Savage. Is that a nickname?"

I didn't want to explain anything about Savage's life that he's not here to share personally, so I just nodded.

She nodded back, and there was nothing more to say. She stood up and looked like she wasn't sure whether to hug me or shake my hand. "Thank you for giving me a glimpse of my son," she said. "I know you didn't know what we are to each other when we made this little delivery plan, but seeing him alive and healthy..." She smiled at me and motioned toward Aurora. "No matter what your history is, no matter what his is, I hope you have a beautiful future."

Tears stung my eyes because I felt like she knew

something that she wouldn't say. That this was the last time she'd see me. That having Savage in my life meant I could never go to the diner again.

I can't unravel the threads of what I've done. I don't fully understand, and all I know is I never, ever meant to hurt anyone.

I finally put Aurora to bed and change into my pajamas. My first night in my new home is nothing like what I'd planned for. But I guess that's life. It always sends you surprises when you least expect them.

But I'm not the woman I used to be.

I'm stronger now. I believe in myself and my ability to weather any storm.

I sit on the couch and light a candle—an old one of Savage's that looks like it's been here for a while. I turn off the lights and fire up my laptop. I put on a playlist of clips from Neon Dawn shows.

Tears fall down my cheeks as I watch the videos I have seen hundreds of times over the last few months. But tonight, the tears are happy tears. Tonight, when my mom looks into the camera and sings about power and love, loss, and fighting, I feel like she's singing just for me.

A text coming into my phone lights up the display, and I grab it.

> Savage: I'm outside. Can I come in?

I don't bother replying to the text. I jump off the couch and rush for the door. I fumble with the locks in the dark, but I open the door to a man who looks wrecked.

Savage's eyes are wild. He looks me over from head to toe, and then he takes a few steps back like he's changing his mind about being here.

"Savage," I say his name with all the apology, affection, and concern I have been building up in my heart all night. I hold the door open with one hand and step onto the front step in my bare feet. "Come here."

He takes a step backward, looks at me, and then surges forward. Under the single porch light, we hug hard, and his chest heaves with emotion. He's not crying, not talking, but his breaths are coming hard and fast, and he just holds me. I cling to him with all my strength, willing to give him everything I have and even what I don't have.

I don't have answers.

I don't have money.

I don't really have options.

But I know now that none of that matters. All that matters is love.

And whether he's willing to see it or not, what I feel for him is real. It's sincere and serious, and I'm going to lean into it for as long as he will let me.

We rock each other back and forth outside until a huge moth dive-bombs my hair, trying to get close to the porch light. Savage swats at it, and then I go inside and he follows. He locks the door behind me, and he doesn't say anything. Just takes my hand, leads me to the couch, and together, we lie down spooning in the fading light of the laptop and my mom's soft music playing on a loop.

When I open my eyes, Savage isn't next to me. He's sitting at the kitchen table reading something on his phone. He looks so strong and yet so vulnerable, all at the same time.

I can't tell if it's morning yet. The baby monitor is playing white noise, and I peek at it and see that Aurora is still fast asleep. I get up and go to the kitchen, looping my arms around Savage's shoulders. I place a kiss on the top of his mussed hair.

"Your father is in a nursing home now," I tell him softly. "Your mom got the job at the diner when she could no longer take care of him. He's stable, and she visits him every couple of days. She has her own friends and life now. She misses you, though. She's so sorry for what she cost you."

He doesn't need me to run interference between him and his mom. I know that. But if he's going to leave me, if I never see him again after today, I want him to know what she shared in the few minutes we talked.

"She blames herself completely," I say, kissing him again. "I would too."

He nods and holds my hands in his. "Do you think," he asks me, his voice low in the dim kitchen, "that I'm going to turn out like him?"

His grip on my hands is so tight, I know it's taking everything he has to form the question.

"Like your dad?" I echo. I move to sit down at the table next to him so I can look at his face, but I grab his hands in mine as soon as I'm seated. "Savage, no. I don't think so. I think men who are violent don't have an interest in finding another way to handle their emotions. Just by asking that question, you've proven that you do. You're your own man—and a better man, I would argue—because of what you've been through."

He looks down at the table, staring off into space. "I went to a job tonight," he tells me. "I brought a weapon. I was planning to hurt people. I wanted—I needed—to hurt people."

I swallow hard at the sudden dryness in my throat. I think about his ribs and how badly he was hurt. I have to wonder if he went out tonight seeking relief or revenge. "What happened?" I ask quietly.

He shakes his head. "Phantom tailed me. He told me to sort my shit out." He chuckles. "He took the fucking bat from my hands and threw it away."

My stomach sinks as I picture Savage, furious and hurting, a baseball bat in his hands. "You didn't use it." It's a statement, not a question.

He nods in agreement.

"No one was hurt," I say.

He nods again. "Yeah, but…"

I grip his hands firmly in mine. "You made the choice."

"Phantom made the choice. I—"

I interrupt him, raising my voice above a whisper. "No, Savage. I don't care that Phantom tossed your stupid bat. You have hands and guns. You could have gone to find the bat, you could have picked up a rock or a brick. You made the choice not to hurt anyone. It's that simple."

"Sometimes I'm not sure I'll make the right choice. I've fucked up so many times." He pulls his hands away from me and drops his face into his hands. "I've screwed up, Claire."

"And so have I. So has your mom. I can't think of a single person I've ever met, except Aurora, who hasn't screwed up a lot of shit. And I know she will. One thing I told myself every day that I was pregnant was that I was never gonna raise my daughter to have false expectations of herself. My momma embraced the mess of life, and she showed me that every day is literally a new dawn."

Savage meets my eyes, and I smile. I'm not even sad talking about this. It's true. "I don't know my real dad. Don't know his name and don't want to. My mom told me she hooked up with so many guys on the road." I laugh. "She had fun. She only got pregnant once, though, and she decided it was a sign to try something new. And she was so, so great at it."

I smooth my new bangs down over my forehead. "But do you think there weren't times when she questioned whether she should have found out who my dad was? That she should have had a solid nine-to-five job instead of playing the bar circuit? I didn't grow up here, but when Mom got too sick to sing, this is where we were, so this is where she stayed. She literally left Neon Dawn one day, rented a house near a hospital, and said, 'This is home now.'"

Savage licks his lips. "Your mom is your ma. That's different."

"How?" I demand. "How is it different?"

His face goes dark, and his eyes fall into shadows. "Could you ever really love a guy like me?"

The question throws me, and I don't hesitate to answer it. "Yes," I insist. "I probably already do, but I don't want you to feel any obligation. This relationship isn't equal. And until I can pull my own weight—"

He waves a hand at me, but I won't stop talking.

"You asked me, Savage. Let me answer."

I get up from the table and wrap my arms around his shoulders. I lean forward and whisper in his ear, "All you need to know is that I trust in the man you are. Not the man you think you should be or the man you might become someday. I trust you, Savage. With my life, my daughter, and my heart."

I let go of him, shaken by what I've revealed. I can't claim this man for my own. I can't promise him a future that I haven't even begun to build. But I can tell him the truth I've come to feel, believe, and see day after day since he bought me from the filthy hands of Mad Dog and the Hellfires.

He sits at the table, looking down into his hands, until, finally, he pushes up and joins me in the living room, taking me in his arms. We don't say more. But I'd like to think that, together, we make a solemn pledge. Not only to each other. But to ourselves. The past is the past, and we are who and what we are.

Today.

Together.

That's all that matters for now.

Savage stays with me for a whole week. During the days, he sits on the floor and plays with Aurora. I make more progress on finding a job and go out only once to the mall with Savage to buy a suit that I can wear for job interviews.

We don't talk about the past.

We don't make promises.

We also don't have sex.

We get to know each other all over again.

We talk about our childhoods—me living on the road with my mom, being homeschooled until seventh grade, when we finally settled down here. How my mom got sick and spent ten years battling her body until she lost the fight.

Savage tells me about the army. What he loved about it. What he hated. How he learned to fight and to kill, and how something inside him hated that he already knew so much about taking a life from living in a home that felt like death every day.

When he opened up to me, I could tell it was the first time he was really processing how terrifying and miserable his childhood was. Yes, he blames his mother on some level for not leaving.. But he also still blames himself for existing, for being the object of his father's endless abuse.

We cooked dinners together, took Aurora on walks, and slept curled together like perfectly nested spoons.

We're walking Aurora one day at a park near the condo when Savage takes my hand. "She's gotta call me something," he says. "I can't have her saying 'Uncle Tank' before she says my name."

I nod, not sure where he's going with this. The afternoon is beautiful, the sun shining. The grass looks impossibly green, and when we stop at the park, Aurora—who is now crawling at Formula 1 speeds—face-plants immediately and then looks back at us before bursting into tears. We both drop to our knees and soothe her, then Savage picks her up and pushes her in the baby swing beside a mom who is giving him a healthy eye-fucking.

I can't blame her. He's gorgeous. He exudes power. And right now, he's sleeping in my bed, recovering like a man healing from his inner wounds, just like he healed from his physical wounds only a few weeks ago. I'd be lying if I said I couldn't wait until he made a decision about what we are to each other.

I've been letting him take the lead, and the question about what Aurora should call him feels like he's leading me someplace.

"Uncle Savage sounds a little too Addams Family," I laugh.

He shakes his head, and I watch the care he takes to push Aurora gently but firmly enough that she giggles with every surge the swing makes higher and higher. "Tank's an uncle. Phantom's an uncle. I don't know what I am to her."

I don't throw out any possibilities. He's a smart man. Aurora will never remember the few months she had with Anthony. I don't know that any man needs to be that father figure in name. The role he plays will be what matters. "Did you have any ideas?" I ask, knowing full well he probably figured it all out before he brought the question up.

"Everything I've thought of is a mouthful. It might take her a while to learn it," he hedges.

"Okay," I say. "Like what?"

He cocks his chin at me and lowers his eyes. "I was thinking Papa Ethan or Papa E. Something short, catchy. Special. Just for her."

Tears immediately spring to my eyes. This isn't anything I'd expected. Maybe Ethan or Sav, a shorter version of Savage. But Papa something?

"E will be a lot easier to say than Tank," I tease.

"Part of my thinking," he teases back, nodding.

When Aurora starts getting fussy, we take her home and put her down for a nap. I head into the kitchen to pour us something cold to drink when I feel Savage behind me. His cock is hard, and he rubs his hips against my rear end.

"What about you, Claire?" he asks, lowering his lips to my hair. "What do you want to call me?"

I turn around so I'm facing him, our hips pressed together. My back is against the counter, and I reach up to wrap my arms around his neck. "I have another E word for you," I murmur, lifting up on my toes to kiss his lips. "You're my salvation, my hero, my best friend, my biker, my lover. You're my *everything*."

He kisses me lightly, anchoring his muscular hands to my waist and picking me up off the floor. I wrap my legs around him as he walks us toward the living room. Aurora's bedroom door is shut, and the noise machine and monitor are on. He takes one look at it and sets me on the couch. Then he points. "Where are we going with this?"

I feel like the question echoes on so many levels. Where are we going with this relationship. This afternoon. This thing between us that feels hardly acknowledged but getting bigger by the day.

"As long as you're going to fuck me senseless, I'll go wherever you are," I tell him.

He growls and I giggle, and then I turn around and face my front toward the back of the couch. Savage gets behind me and tugs the waistband of my shorts past my rear end, tossing my panties with them.

He leaves on my top and bra, and I hear him unzip his jeans and shimmy them down.

He reaches between my legs, and his long, thick fingers part my curls. He leans close to me and murmurs in my ear. "Claire, I want to go where you are. Where your baby girl is. I want to be a part of all of this, even if I don't know how."

I nod and bend forward, pivoting my hips and ass toward him. "Savage," I pant, my core growing hot at the promise of him inside me. "I need you. I want you every way I can get you."

He pulls his hand from my slick pussy and lines up his hips behind me. I grab the back of the couch for balance as I feel him slide the head of his cock between my legs. He strokes my pussy, wetting every single inch of me before touching my clit with his shaft.

Electric currents of pleasure ricochet through my body and weaken my legs. I grip the back of the couch with all my strength and stretch my back toward him, desperately craving that fullness, that thrust from him that will send every nerve ending into pure bliss.

But he teases me, stroking and sliding in just the tip, wetting his dick, stroking my clit with his shaft, and working my poor pussy into a desperate, needy frenzy. My nipples harden inside my bra, and the friction of my flesh against the fabric has me risking touching myself. I don't want to smash my face on the couch, but I need more, so much more.

I slip a hand under my tank top and tug at my bra cups, freeing my nipples. Then I drag the fabric of the tank down so my breasts are totally exposed, hanging in front of me as I wiggle and press against Savage.

"Fuck," he grunts, bending low at the waist to lean forward and grab one nipple between his fingers. "Claire, you make me so hard. You make me fucking crazy with need."

"Fuck me," I beg. "I need to feel you, Savage.

Please." I'm rocking my hips back and lowering my chest to get closer to the fingers working my nipple. My body is numb and alive, taut and poised precariously, but I don't care. Just like my heart, I'm willing to risk it all for this bliss, for this love, for this man.

Instead of sliding inside me, though, he turns me around, seats me on the couch, and hooks his hand under the bend of my knee. I have to scooch to the edge of the couch, and he eventually has to drop to his knees on the floor to line up my body with his, but we finally get there. When he thrusts his cock deep inside me, I have to smash my eyes closed and clutch the couch cushions to hold back my screams.

He feels better than good. I lose all sense of space and time as he slides inside me, going fully balls deep, banging the head of his cock deep inside my walls. When he slides out, he teases my swollen clit with the tip of his erection, and sparks of light erupt behind my eyes.

I work my hips, grinding myself against his body. Finally, he stops pulling in and out, just thrusts deep and releases, faster and harder until I can't tell if he ever leaves my body.

We're locked together in a rhythm of fucking and grinding until my climax climbs my body like a runner making it over the finish line after a marathon.

I'm panting, sweating, shaking, and riding every second of the waves of pleasure.

My breasts tremble, and Savage tweaks one of my nipples, like cranking up my pleasure as I ride the wave of my climax. My knees fall open as I lose control of my legs, and Savage stands up, lifts my knees so my ass comes fully up off the couch, and bangs me hard until he's roaring out his pleasure.

I cry out on every exhale, the pleasure so exquisite, the boneless sense of being at the mercy of his ability to satisfy me so completely, I give in fully. There's no hesitation. Just his body, mine, and the total ecstasy of our lovemaking.

After he comes, he slowly sets my ass down on the couch. His eyes are closed, and his hair is drenched with sweat. It's then that I realize he came inside me—again. No better safe than sorry this time. I still haven't gotten my period, but no matter what happens, with Savage, I know I'm safe. I am absolutely sure, in a way I've never been sure about anything before, that I'll never, ever be sorry.

FIFTEEN
SAVAGE

I DON'T GO BACK to the compound, but I do show up at a job. I've stayed on the secure messaging app we use to plan our gigs, so I know where and when shit's going down. This is a deal that Shadow has been working on for a couple of months as part of the effort to get involved in more legit businesses.

Now that he's got an old lady and Phantom has a whole load of kids to take care of, plus the one on the way, we've been trying to find sources of revenue that are lower-risk. Cash-heavy businesses where we can wash money we pick up from gambling or security gigs, shit like that.

Shadow met with a woman who owns a chain of nail salons—three in total across the area. She got herself deep into debt, and Shadow thought it'd be the perfect business to buy out—if the owner will agree to our terms.

We're meeting the woman at a small diner far on the outskirts of town. Shadow's gonna present the offer while Phantom and I hover in the background, making sure nothing goes wrong.

This lady owes money to some shady people, so getting involved means we'd tangle with yet another enemy. If we're gonna take on the risk, we need everything to go according to plan.

I roll up to the meeting where Shadow is dressed like he's going to court. I look him up and down, from his weird boat shoes to his khaki pants and pink golf shirt.

"I know your woman didn't buy you those clothes because Violet's got better taste than that." I eyeball his entire getup. "But whose grandpa did you knock over to get those shoes?"

I clap him hard on the back in greeting, and he curses me out in my ear. "Asshole. Good to see you."

I'm dressed in a forgettable outfit, but nothing that screams I borrowed clothes from the airport lost and found like Shadow. Phantom rolls up a few minutes later like me. Plain, solid-color T-shirt, no logos, long-sleeved shirt unbuttoned over it to hide our tatts, and dark jeans.

He gives me a look when he sees me, then a curt nod. "Savage," he says. And that's it. No lecture, no catch-up. He said not to come back until my head was right, and I think, I hope, that I'm there.

Phantom and I stake the place out, our trucks

strategically positioned in the lot while Shadow, who is calling himself Jim for this meeting, and the owner of the string of nail places, Marybeth, sit in a booth right by a massive glass window. The plan is to make sure she wasn't followed and that she's not part of any kind of a scam herself.

We're supposed to deliver her a ten-grand advance in cash tonight, and in exchange, she'll sign an amendment to the corporate documents that she filed with the state of Florida to add a trust our club attorney set up as the majority owner of the salons. That signature won't mean shit unless it's done in front of a notary, so she's agreed to hire one to meet Jim at the diner to do the deal.

This could be a much easier deal, but Marybeth is a cool six figures in debt to her loan shark and is already three days late on the last extension they gave her to make a payment of at least twenty-five grand. From what she told us, she's afraid she's being tailed, and all she wants is to get out from under her debt and get out of the state with her face intact.

Meeting us in a public place means, if she's being tailed, we'll get eyes on the asshole she owes the money to while making sure nothing too dangerous goes down. Loan sharks are lazy and their collection agents might be willing to get their hands dirty, but they sure as fuck don't like public messes.

We could have paid her guys outright, just given her the money to clear the debt and then bought out the salons, but we didn't trust her to just pay off the assholes if we gave her the money.

Marybeth's afraid for her life and basically agreed to everything except telling us who she owed money to unless we gave her a seed fund to abandon the salons and get the hell out of town. She said once she no longer legally owned the businesses and could get far away, we could step in and pay off her debt using her salon manager as a front woman and then take over ownership of all three locations.

It should have been an easy transaction. But as soon as Shadow goes into the diner and sits, my Spidey senses start tingling. I text Phantom on our secure app.

> Me: I don't care how well Shadow vetted this. Something seems off.

I only have to wait a couple seconds before he replies.

> Phantom: I know. You packin'?

I'm not. All my guns are at the compound, safely far away from Aurora and my recent outburst of rage.

> Me: No.

I'm trying to figure out why I feel like shit. Why none of this is sitting right. I keep an eye on Shadow, and sure enough, he's talking like a time-share salesman to Marybeth. She keeps looking toward the diner door, no doubt waiting for her notary to come through.

I look away from the windows and scan the parking lot when a faded orange, rusted, shitstain of a pickup truck catches my eye. I process it in slow motion, realizing it looks familiar, and that's when I feel a sick sensation climbing up my throat.

Mad Dog.

That's fucking Mad Dog's truck. I scan the lot, my pulse ratcheting up in my chest. I don't see any bikes or signs of trouble, but Shadow started talking with this lady just days or weeks after the deal went down with Mad Dog. It's gotta be him, and he's gotta be involved.

I don't know what the fuck is going on here, but there's no way this is a coincidence. Something big is going down, and I sure as fuck don't like surprises—especially these kinds of surprises.

I go into the group chat and text both Shadow and Phantom. Viper and Blade, our club treasurer, are in the chat too. Blade's been on the money stuff every step of the way, and Viper's prepared to show up if we need backup. We just might.

> Me: Abort. Hellfires on site.

I notice Shadow's shoulders pick up inside, and he raises a finger to Marybeth, while he excuses himself to check his phone. I've got one leg out of the truck, my boot planted on the asphalt, when I'm kicked sideways in the left knee. I curse to the holy heavens and drop to my side, rolling to absorb the shock of falling.

"Always trying to be the hero," a familiar voice sneers.

I'm on my back, looking up into an already dark Florida sky and into the filthy cowboy hat of Mad Dog. "What the fuck do you want, shit-for-brains? You starting something you're ready to finish here?"

Mad Dog laughs and flicks open a knife with a blade about five inches long. It's a filthy weapon, rusty and dirt-marred on the handle, but I can tell the point is sharp enough to do real damage.

I know Shadow is someplace inside that diner, and Phantom should still be in his truck. For now, this is between Mad Dog and me. I decide to play up the injury to my knee, so I fake trying to struggle to get up and suck air.

"Goddamn," I groan. I was never one for theater in school, but Mad Dog seems more intent on staring at Shadow than worrying about me. I'm on the ground between my truck and another parked car. Nobody inside that diner is going to see him if he decides to bend down and gut me like a fish or put a boot to my nuts.

My mind races, and I think long and hard about what he wants. "You in on this deal?" I ask him. "You the one who's got a note on that debt?"

Mad Dog spits tobacco through his teeth, and it lands on the leg of my jeans. "Stupid little shit," Mad

Dog says. "Don't ask questions you don't want to know the answers to."

Thankfully, he is predictable as well as distracted, so when he rears back to plant one of those boots in my gut, I roll onto my side. He reacts fast, but I'm faster, and I kick out with my right foot, trip his ass to the ground, and make a play for his knife.

What happens next is a blur of cursing and fists. I'm hitting him, dodging blows, and trying to make sure the knife, which he took a punch to the belly in order to grab, doesn't land in a place that's gonna make me bleed.

I hear motion around us, and suddenly Phantom's behind Mad Dog, his arms locking him tight in a choke hold. Phantom hisses in Mad Dog's ear, "What the fuck is this? You trying to start a war, you worthless little prick?"

"The only worthless prick is this piece of shit. The one who thought he could buy my niece and my brother's bitch."

When he refers to Claire and Aurora, just the fact that he's even thinking about them anymore, my sight goes red. I haul off and punch him in the gut so many times, he doubles over and spits a thick stream of bloody spittle onto the ground.

I grab the knife from his weak hand just as Shadow comes running up.

"Shit's off," he says, his voice low. "Deal's not happening. That bitch played me."

He registers slowly that Phantom's holding Mad Dog and I've got the asshole's knife in my hand.

"Savage," Shadow says. "Think about what you're doing."

Shadow's hands are in the air, and he's giving me the "put it down" sign. My heart is pumping hard, adrenaline urging me to finish this fuck. Put this knife through Mad Dog's heart and end whatever this is once and for all.

"We said," I seethe, talking so close to this asshole's face that I knock the cowboy hat off his head with mine, "that deal was over. Concluded, all in. No loose ends. You got seller's regret, that's your problem."

I look around, curious why there are no other Hellfires here. "What'd you do?" I demand. "Think you were gonna shake us down for a couple of extra Gs?"

Just then, the diner doors open, and we hear the clack of heels clomping toward us.

Phantom makes the call. "No witnesses," he says. I open the back door of my truck, and Phantom shoves Mad Dog in. Shadow gets in the other side, so both my brothers are flanking Mad Dog. Then I get behind the wheel, and we take off. I make sure I run that fucking skanky cowboy hat under my wheels as we leave.

"Where to?" I ask.

"I didn't know the fucking Heat were running a car service. Times must be tough for you boys." Mad Dog's gaining his breath back, but I'll bet I busted a few ribs. I can tell from the strain in his voice he's hurting deep.

"Shut your mouth unless you plan to explain."

Shadow's about to lose his cool. His eyes are bugged wide open, and his nostrils are flaring. "What the fuck do you have to do with this deal?"

"There ain't no deal," Mad Dog says. I look in the rearview mirror and see Phantom and Shadow exchange looks.

"That's bullshit," Shadow snaps. "I've been working this for months. The salons are legit. Marybeth is the owner. She's eyeballs deep in debt."

"When I'm not balls deep fucking her," Mad Dog drawls. "You think it's that hard to sell a woman-in-distress story to you assholes?" He laughs. "Fuck all y'all."

Then it hits me, and I think it hits Shadow too at the same time. Mad Dog set us up. A long play for a little bit of cash. The problem is not just that he almost scammed us out of ten grand—now he knows we're trying to go legit. That we've got our eyes on other ways to make clean money and wash the dirty shit.

Maybe this wasn't about Claire at all. Maybe this was about nothing more than spying on the competition, Hellfires-style. Whatever it is, he didn't get our money, but he's wasted months of Shadow's time and made us look like fools.

"What're we gonna do with him?" Phantom asks.

And I know what he's asking. Last year, Phantom had to make a tough call. Whether to snuff out a prospect who betrayed us. Lied to us. Played Phantom and all the rest of us for fools. It would have been so easy to put a bullet in the kid's head and push his bike into the ocean. But Phantom was the one to make the call.

We get our hands dirty, but there's some blood that can never be washed off. Murder's a business we've been able to stay clear of. At least so far.

Phantom looks to me. "Savage?"

I feel bad making the call, but I know if we leave Mad Dog alive, that's a loose end for Claire. If we take him out now, Marybeth would only have to make one phone call to the cops and Shadow's face would be on every wanted poster in the Sunshine State.

"Get his phone," I say. Phantom and Shadow work their way through his pockets, and Shadow holds the knife to Mad Dog's throat until he reluctantly unlocks the phone.

"Send Marybeth a text," I say, heading the truck toward Port Tampa Bay. Mad Dog grunts and looks fearful for the first time since he kicked out my knee. Only now is the adrenaline starting to wear off and I can feel the deep ache. I'll be lucky if I can walk tomorrow. "Tell your bitch that you're safe and you got the money. That you're going underground for a while and you'll be in touch."

He tries to yank his phone away from Phantom, but Phantom tut-tuts at him, while Shadow traces the tip of the knife along the asshole's Adam's apple. "Go on," Shadow seethes. "You think I'm afraid of cleaning what'll be left of you off these seats? Try me."

Mad Dog grunts, and Phantom watches as he texts exactly what I told him to say. Then he clicks send.

"Now what, motherfuckers?" Mad Dog's got balls, I'll give him that.

"You willing to spend some of that cash to buy us a short-term solution?" I meet Phantom's eyes in the rearview mirror.

He's my brother, so I expect him to have my back. He doesn't surprise me.

"Count out five Gs," I tell Shadow. "This asshat's going on a boat ride."

Three hours later, we're out five grand, but one of our contacts at the port was happy to take the envelope of cash as payment for transporting a passenger on a cargo ship.

We ran over his phone with the truck and tossed the pieces, along with his knife, into the Gulf, then wished Mad Dog a happy trip and left him to his two-week journey overseas. Assuming he can figure out a way back—and afford the trip—we won't have to worry about Mad Dog for, by my estimate, a solid month or two. If this little stunt isn't enough to teach him not to mess with the Heat, I'll be ready when he's back in town.

"We're gonna need to find another arms dealer," Phantom says when we get back to the diner. "Can't say that bothers me much."

I shake my head. "Who knows. Those assholes ain't like us. Without Anthony and Mad Dog beating sense into the crew, they might fall apart in the time it takes Mad Dog to find his way back to the States. Some of them might even try to prospect for us."

Phantom shakes his head, then claps a hand on Shadow's shoulder. "Shit happens," he says. "Let it go."

Shadow's face is dark, and I know he's questioning every minute of every conversation he had with Marybeth. What he missed. How he missed it. We'll have to debrief later and figure out what our next moves are, but fuck. We lost five grand and got rid of a little problem we didn't even know we had.

"I'm sorry that shit came back to bite us," I tell Phantom. "You specifically warned me not to let that happen."

Phantom shrugs. "She's one of us now, I'm thinking. Ain't she?" He stares at me through intensely dark eyes. "We protect our own."

I nod, finally admitting it out loud. To my brothers. To myself. "She's mine," I tell them, even though I'm not sure I've said the words to her. "She's one of us."

Phantom nods, then claps me on the shoulder. He gets in his truck and heads back toward the compound, leaving Shadow and me alone. I can tell my brother is shaken, pissed.

"Let it go," I tell him. "You got scammed. It happens to the best of us."

Shadow shakes his head and scrubs his hands over his head. "This is fucking with me, man," he says. "I thought I knew her. I did the research, the site visits, observation. How'd I get it so, so wrong?"

"I don't know," I tell him. "But does it matter? You got preyed on. Mad Dog set out to scam us out of money because he thought the Heat was an easy mark due to something I did. If anyone should feel like shit, I should."

Shadow's lost in thought. I can understand how he feels. He did something he thought was right, was good for the club. And it had disastrous consequences. There's a chance the Hellfires club won't make it through losing both Anthony and Mad Dog. But if they do, Mad Dog's gonna come back and be out for blood.

"I'm gonna go home and fuck my wife," he finally says, unbuttoning the sleeves of his pink shirt.

"Change those fucking shoes," I holler at him. "But save them. I might want to borrow them for my next knitting circle."

Shadow gives me the finger and grins, then peels out of the lot.

I've been thinking a lot the last week that I've been alone with Claire. About what she means to me. What Aurora means to me.

I may have told Phantom she's mine, but I don't think I'll be able to give myself to someone until I close a few more doors to my past.

"Table for one, sir?" The teenage hostess looks me up and down and then points to the counter. "Or do you want a seat at the counter?"

"Put me in Val's section." I check the time on my phone.

"She's gonna go off shift in about ten minutes," the

teenager says, looking confused. "Do you still want to be seated in her section?"

I nod. "Yep."

She grabs a menu. "Right this way."

I follow her, keeping my eyes on the floor. The busy carpet gives me something to focus on while I steady my nerves.

As soon as the girl seats me, I open the menu and start scanning the pages, even though I know there's no way I could eat right now.

"Hi there, hon, what can I get started for you?" A glass of water and a napkin-wrapped roll of silverware are placed on the table in front of me. It's obvious she's using her work voice, and she hasn't noticed me behind the menu.

I'm suddenly overcome with nerves. My hands start to shake, and I suck my lower lip into my mouth and bite down hard. When I don't say anything, she leans closer.

She sees me then. Really sees me.

"Ethan? Oh, honey. I never expected to see you again."

There is a catch in Mom's voice, and I put down the menu, unable to say a word.

"Can you sit?" I motion toward the opposite side of the booth.

She nods. "Let me clock out. I'll be back in two minutes. Please, honey. Wait here for me."

I'm not going anywhere, but I nod to let her know I heard her. Once she's gone, I'm so frantic and frazzled, I don't know what to do. I pick up my phone and send Claire a text.

> Me: I'm at the diner. Came to talk to my mother. It's been twelve years.

I get a response immediately.

> Claire: Do you need me? Should I get there? Are you okay?

I read the words and realize that's all I need from her. To know that she'd drop everything and come here. To know that she'd be here just to support me. I don't know if I'm okay with seeing my mom, but I'm very okay with everything else right now.

I got rid of Mad Dog—at least for now. And I've got Claire and Aurora waiting for me at home. Home used to be a dirty word. A word that reminded me of my father. My mother. That house. The fists.

I only ever call the compound the compound, but now, I might have a chance. A real chance to make a life. I just need a few answers so I can trust that I won't screw it up.

My hands are still sweating when Val slides into the booth across from me. She's brought us both coffee.

"I hope you still drink coffee," she says, and immediately, tears spring to her eyes. "You look great, Ethan. I want to know everything. Absolutely everything you're willing to share." She lowers her head and looks at her hands. "And of course, if you're not here for that, I'm willing to listen to anything you have to say to me."

She wipes her cheeks and sniffles back the sadness. Then she raises her chin and swallows. "I've changed a little. Maybe not enough. Over the years you've been gone, I told myself that if I ever got the chance to see you again, I would accept whatever punishment you wanted to impose. The harsh words, more years of silence." She swallows hard again and clears her throat. "Go on, son. I'll listen. No matter what you need to say, I can take it."

Can take it?

I cock my head in confusion, and I lean forward across the table. "Mom, I have some questions, for sure. But the only harsh words I have to say to you are I'm sorry for not being better. For not being enough. I wanted to save you, but I chose to save myself. I'm so, so sorry."

Her mouth opens, and it's the same mouth I remember forming an O when I left. Frowning when I cried. Smiling when she took care of me.

"You're apologizing to me? Ethan, when you had to leave the military, I thought I was going to die from the pain. That happened to you because of me. Because I chose your father over you. Because I wouldn't leave. I owe you the apology."

I shake my head.

All these years, I've blamed myself for leaving my mother with him. Yes, it cost me everything, but I had peace. I had freedom. No one hit me unless I punched first. No one insulted me, shut me into a corner. I found a family of misfits and losers where I fit in just right. But all that time, I never forgot that I had a mother whom I loved more than anything just a few miles away. A mother I left to a living hell.

We talk for the next four hours. We order dinner and dessert. I text Claire to let her know where I am and when I'll be home. I text her so she'll know that I'm thinking of her. So she'll know I'm all right. And for the first time in twelve years, I think I truly am.

SIXTEEN
CLAIRE

I CAN'T HELP but check my phone every few minutes while Savage is gone. I had no idea where he was going when he went to work today, but finding out he's spending a couple hours with his mother has my heart in a tailspin.

I try to distract myself with my own good news, but it seems like such a tiny thing compared to whatever he's got going on. After I put Aurora to bed, I take a shower and put on my pajamas. I climb onto the couch with my laptop and plan to do a little research, but there's a knock at the front door.

I set my laptop on the kitchen counter, then run to the front door. Savage stands under the porch light, looking brighter somehow. A lightness emanates from him, and it makes me smile.

"We really need to get you your own key. But I'm not sure we've reached that stage in our relationship."

He swoops through the door and picks me up in his

arms. He spins me around once, and then he sets me down and holds me so tight I can feel the beating of his heart through his dark T-shirt.

"Hm," I hum against his chest. "You feel so good."

He releases me and laces his fingers through mine. "God, babe, I've got so much to tell you." He looks toward the closed bedroom door. "Aurora sleeping?"

I nod. "She's out. I tried to get her to stand tonight after dinner, and those little legs are tired. You guys have a good day?"

Savage isn't normally one for small talk. We sit together on the couch, and I rest my bare legs over his lap. "Yeah, babe. Everything is good."

I cup his cheek with a hand and look into his face. "Are you okay?"

He nods, but then he takes my hand and kisses the top of each finger. "I've got some good news and some not-so-great news. Bad news first?"

I sniff, drawing a deep breath in through my nose. I wasn't expecting any bad news. I hope it doesn't have to do with his dinner with his mother. "Okay," I tell him. "What happened?"

He doesn't give me a lot of details, but he does explain that Mad Dog tried to scam the club out of money. My face burns hot with rage and shame, and I feel a little fight kick up in my chest.

"That asshole," I say, wishing I could fight him, fight back, but Savage chuckles.

"He won't be a problem for a while."

I search Savage's body for injuries, but he looks fine

besides a barely noticeable limp, so I'm thankful he didn't get hurt. And Mad Dog's clearly not dead, but I trust that he won't be a problem if Savage says he won't be.

He tells me about his chat with his mother, but instead of telling me all the details, he pulls me into his lap. "I want to tell you something, baby."

I wrap my arms around him and rest my head on his shoulder. I brace myself for whatever it is his mama said. I hope it's nothing bad, but it's impossible to feel fear when I'm on Savage's lap. Besides, he said he had good news and bad news, and I am darn sure Mad Dog trying to scam the Heat is not the good news.

I take a deep breath, and Savage's scent, the heat of his skin, fills my senses and lulls me into deep relaxation. I wiggle my toes and rub my head against him, stupidly happy and light. I don't even know what he has to say, but he could tell me he wants to watch paint dry, and I think I'd be delighted.

"Claire," he says, his voice not tentative or shaking, "I'm falling in love with you. I think I've known from the moment I met you that I wanted to make you mine. But I've been so goddamn scared that I would screw it up. That my anger, that my past, my blood, for fuck's sake, would show up like a ticking time bomb in my soul someday and ruin everything. I didn't want to do that to you. I don't want that for myself. So, I stuffed my feelings down where they couldn't get out."

I lift my face and study his as he speaks. His lips curve into a smile, and his eyes are so warm, it's like

I'm seeing the real him for the first time. "Savage, I—" I try to interrupt, but he silences me with a finger against my lips.

"One more thing," he says. "I am devoted to Aurora too. I love and care about her. But I know if I were you, it'd take me a long time before I'd trust anyone with my baby girl. I'm stubborn, Claire. I didn't speak to my mother for twelve years because I thought she blamed me for…" He shakes his head. "Point is, I'm willing to wait as long as it takes to build a relationship with your daughter. You're a package deal, and I want you both."

I can hardly process what I'm hearing.

Four months ago, I was trapped in a loveless situation with a man who talked with his fists and yelled with his voice. After he passed, I thought for sure I'd be dead or on the streets by now.

But Savage came along and saved me—and maybe, just maybe, I've saved him in some way too.

I stroke the stubble on his chin and ask the question that's been on my mind. "Do you want to talk about what happened with your mom?"

I ask the question, but my voice breaks because Savage is starting to massage my thighs. His strong fingers knead my muscles, and the sensation warms my entire body from toes to cheeks. I'm smiling, relaxing into his touch, when he says in a low and gravelly voice, "I need time to process everything."

I can understand that. Everything about life, I think, is a process. Forgiveness is a process. Maturity is a process. Parenting, relationships, career. Even getting to know yourself—it's all time and effort. A process that I'm learning requires kindness. Especially directed toward ourselves.

"So, I have a little good news too." I lean back against the couch cushions and let Savage work his fingers down my calves, his fingers releasing little sparks of pleasure with every squeeze.

"What's that, baby?" He's looking me over with a completely new expression.

I love that look that makes me think he's imagining all the things he wants to do to me. But something has lifted from his shoulders too.

The side of his mouth curls playfully, and the corners of his eyes crinkle.

"I have a job interview."

He moves my legs off his lap and moves closer to me. "No shit? Holy fuck. Where? With who? That's great news." He seems swept up in my excitement, but then all of a sudden, the reality seems to set in. "Wait, though. What about Aurora? Who's gonna watch her if you're working?" He shakes his head, his brow lowered in concern. "Claire, maybe you shouldn't work. Maybe you should stay home and just take care of her for a while."

I lean forward and cup his face in my hands. "Savage," I say firmly. "It's an interview. I don't have a job offer. And I don't know what I'm going to do about any of that yet. There's day care and babysitters."

He shakes his head. "You'd trust strangers with her? Fuck that. I—"

My grin stops him short.

"What?" he asks.

"I trusted you," I remind him. "And Poppy, Stella, Tank, and Phantom. The list goes on. I don't trust anyone with my baby, but we can't hide out here in this condo forever."

He swallows hard and scrubs a hand over his face roughly. "I don't like it," he admits. "It scares me, thinking about leaving her with anyone but you."

I suck my lower lip into my mouth and bite back tears. This is how I know he loves us. Not by his words. Not by the many, many actions over the last few months that have shown me he cares. But by the fact that he is worried. Suffering inside because he wants what's best for Aurora.

I rest my forehead against his and take his hands. "We'll figure it out when the time comes. Together, okay? You'll be part of any decision I make. As long as you want to be a part of it."

"Fuck yes," he says. "Forever. Always."

Whether he means that in a literal sense or not, I don't care. I lower my lips to his and start kissing him, hungrily, my mouth wanting to express all the feelings I have been suppressing all this time.

No one knows the future—God knows, I get that—but he's here. He's been here. And he wants to be here. And I am going to make the most of every minute I can love this man.

We're making out like kids then, our lips rough as I bite his chin, lick the hollow of his neck. I'm hot from the inside out, flames of desire raging within me now that I can set everything free—love, lust, and hope.

But Savage cups my face and stops me, both of us breathless. "Babe, wait. What's the job interview?"

"Poppy's mom," I say, refusing to be distracted. I reach for his waistband and unbuckle his belt. "She works in local government and has a lot of contacts. Poppy wants us to meet so she can network with me, help me find any openings. But she wants to interview me herself for an admin position. She said it's just a temp job while their current admin has knee surgery, but if it works out, she can be a reference for me while I'm looking for something permanent."

I've yanked on Savage's waistband and gotten him to stand up so I can unzip his jeans.

"Babe," he breathes. "That's fucking awesome."

I kneel in front of him and tug his pants and boxer briefs down. His cock is hard, and I grasp it lightly in my hand while I help him step out of his pants. I brush my lips over the head of cock and smile. "Thank you."

Then I lick his shaft, sucking and kissing his erection until his knees buckle. I love his body. The way it feels under my hands. The sounds he makes, the roughness of his callused palms, the softness of his neck, the tender skin around his upper lip, the hypersensitive parts of him that come alive under my mouth.

"Fuck, Claire." He weaves his fingers through my hair and guides my mouth deeper.

I take his length into my mouth, licking and wetting his shaft with long, hard flicks of my tongue. He hums his pleasure as I hum against his cock. He widens his legs, and I work my mouth over him, letting him lightly thrust into my mouth while I relax my throat and shoulders and take all he's able to give.

I groan and murmur, buzzing my tongue over his hardness until he stills and tries to pull out. "Claire, I'm gonna—"

But I don't let him move. I clamp my lips around his shaft and fuck him with my mouth, cupping his balls and fingering the delicate seam underneath.

"Holy fuck!" he roars, his hips thrusting hard against me, my lips swollen from the effort of keeping my mouth on him as he works out his pleasure. "Baby."

He spews his load against my tongue, the hot liquid salty and slightly sweet. I swallow it down and keep bobbing my neck, fucking him through his climax. When he finally stops moving and wobbles on weak knees, I push him back onto the couch.

"I haven't been able to stop thinking about you sucking me here on the couch," I whisper.

His eyes are shut, and his head is thrown back against the cushion. "Come and get it, babe."

I strip off all my clothes, grinning because he manages to wink open one eye and watch me. Until I get to my panties. Then both eyes fly open, and his lips part.

"I could eat you for every meal and never get full," he tells me.

I love the sound of that. Just the idea of his mouth on my sensitive skin sends a flood of wetness to my core. I reach between my legs and touch myself, my nipples going hard and my eyelids feeling heavy.

"Nuh-uh," he says. "Mine." He claps a hand on his thigh, and I pad over to the couch and sit on his lap.

I line up my breasts with his face, and he cups one in each hand. He lightly kisses my sternum, then flicks his hot tongue up to the hollow of my neck. "This was amazing before. But, baby," he says, "things feel different."

It feels that way for me too. It's like we're both unburdened in a way that makes everything easier.

Us is a real thing now, and it's easy.

Together is a real thing now, and it's easy.

Falling in love with each other... That's real too, and it's never felt this easy or this right.

He steals every rational thought from my brain the second he runs the pads of his thumbs over my nipples. "Do you know how fucking delicious these are?" he asks. "I dream about you, about your body. The way you taste, the way you smell." He lowers his mouth to my nipple and sucks one into his mouth. He swirls his tongue around the tip to wet it, then releases it with a loud pop.

Something new and even more exhilarating surges through my body when he tastes me. It's like, deep in my soul, I know I can trust this man. I know I can be myself fully and freely. The prisoner who's been locked down for far too long is set free. But I'm not the newly escaped prisoner I was when Savage rescued me.

Now I'm strong, healthy, walking side by side with

the man I choose and the man who's choosing me. I'm finally and truly free.

I lean into Savage and hug his head to my chest. I'm sure he can feel the rapid pounding of my heart, but maybe he just thinks it's his amazing breast play. Because, my God, this man knows how to lick me.

He laps the flat of his tongue against my hard peak, and a scatter storm of fire dances along my limbs. Then he takes the tip of his tongue and traces circles around my areola, his hands gripping my hips and ass. I feed him my breast, throw my head back, and lose myself to the pleasure.

I slam my eyes shut and see every color of the rainbow behind my lids. We whimper each other's names. We sigh and moan, breathe and take breaks to kiss and tug each other's hair.

When I'm so wet and needy I can hardly stand the ache deep in my core, I feel Savage's cock roar back to life. He's hard beneath me, and I lift my hips, then set myself down on his shaft.

He curses and works his hands up the back of my neck and through my hair, and I keep rubbing him, my pussy growing hotter and more swollen, my nipples aching as he lowers his face to nibble my peaks while I move along his body.

We're locked together like that, scratching an eternal itch, until I have to have him inside me.

I can feel my heartbeat in every inch of my body, my pussy pulsing and my core clamoring for release. I lift my hips and nudge just the head of his cock inside me, and the sensation is so take-my-breath-away good, I cry out his name.

His head is still thrown back against the cushions, but his eyes are wide open and watching, his lips parted. He's as beautiful to me now as the first day I met him, but now there is so much more I see when I look at him. A man who's facing his demons. A man who loves enough to try. A man whom I have gone from doubting to needing to caring for to wanting.

I lower myself onto his cock and feel him slide up my walls. His length hits a spot deep inside me that threatens to send me over the edge, but I'm greedy now. I have what I want, and I need to savor it, savor him.

I roll my hips slowly. The friction of our bodies works my clit and my G-spot all at the same time, and I lift and lower myself, rock and thrust, until I have to stop, have to still my legs and let the exquisite climax take over.

"Savage, fuck." I claw at his shoulders, wanting him closer, deeper, harder, softer. Everything and all of him at once. I unleash my passion on his body, whimpering his name as I ride every crest, and then he's coming again, shuddering and thrusting and pulling me harder onto his cock.

We're sweating and writhing, forcing ourselves as close together as two separate humans can be, until finally, we slow down, ease our way from the heights and depths of our shared pleasure. I collapse against his chest and rest my cheek against his shoulder. He laces his arms around my waist, and we sit there, naked, sweating, and satisfied.

I feel a rush of fluid and don't want to stain his couch, so I get up, peck him on the cheek, and pad to the bathroom. I sit on the toilet, and when I go to clean myself up, I'm shocked to see blood.

My period? I haven't had a period in months. And since Savage and I haven't always been safe about preventing a pregnancy, I know now that I'm fertile again. But this means more than I'm fertile. I'm healthy. I'm coming back to myself. I'm going to be okay.

Thankfully, I bought a few tampons and some pads when I shopped for groceries last time, just in case. I clean myself up, pop in a tampon, and tuck the string out of sight. I walk back into the living room and slip on my clothes.

Savage groans. "No. Naked. Only naked."

I laugh at his slurred words. "Are you drunk on orgasms, babe?" He did have two, and it sounds like he's so completely drained that he can't even speak straight.

"I dunno. Don't care." He grins and keeps his eyes closed but opens his arms. I sit on the couch with him, and we settle in to cuddle.

"Savage," I say quietly. "I have more kind of good news. I just got my period back."

His eyes fly open. "No shit. Just now?"

I nod. "That means we'll have to be safer if we don't want to be, you know... Sorry."

He wraps his arms tighter around me. "Not sorry,"

he says. "Never sorry. But let's be safe for a while. I am hardly used to one kid. I don't think I can handle two yet."

He closes his eyes, and we hold each other until he's snoozing lightly. My bed is just a few feet away, but I stay where I am, thinking, letting my mind travel.

I have a safe home.

A safe relationship.

A promising future.

It took a shit-ton of pain to get here. I've been through things I don't know that I'd ever wish on my worst enemy. I have a lot of time to make up with my daughter. I need to take care of myself again and put the stress of Anthony and the past behind me.

But now, right here and right now, I have something that I haven't felt since I lost my mom.

Peace.

EPILOGUE
SAVAGE

SIX MONTHS LATER...

I roll over onto my side, and my hard cock rubs against Claire's bare ass. I check the time on my phone and then slide my hands over Claire's back. I trace my fingers lightly up her spine, and she shivers, then mumbles, still deep in sleep.

We have to get moving in about an hour, and that means we have just enough time.

I lower my lips to her neck and shove her thick, chestnut hair aside. "Mornin', baby."

We both slept naked, and her small, firm breasts are fully exposed when I move the sheet aside. I reach around her and feel her nipples, soft and relaxed in sleep, wake up under my touch. Claire nudges her ass against my hard cock, and I moan. "Babe," I say. "We gotta get up in like an hour."

"Hm. An hour."

I feel her roll her hips against my erection, and I

know she's more than awake enough for this. I stick my fingers into my mouth to wet them, then slide my leg between Claire's thighs. I find her clit easily. That little nub and I are very good friends, and she comes out to greet me with the tiniest touch.

"You horny, baby?" I ask, teasing her. "You want more of this?" I remove my fingers from between her legs and get an annoyed whimper in response. "Don't worry. I got you."

I roll her onto her back and draw her nipple deep into my mouth. I suck it hard, then soft, and blow hot kisses along her breasts. Once she's wide awake, her lips open and her nipples achingly hard, I part her legs and widen her knees.

There are so many ways I want to love Claire. In our bed. Over the back of the couch. In the truck when Aurora falls asleep on long drives, but eating Claire's pussy in our bed has to be one of my favorites. Her wetness tastes sweet, and her body is so expressive, moving and changing in response to my every touch. I know what to do, I know how she likes it, and I love giving her what she needs.

I slip two fingers inside her and take my sweet time suckling her clit. She can come more than once, so I don't bother saving her orgasms for fucking.

This morning, we have time for at least two. She whispers my name and widens her legs, gripping her knees in her hands, and that's my sign she's close. I pick up the pace with my fingers while slowing down the pace on her clit but applying more pressure with my tongue. She comes apart so, so fast, her pussy spasming against my mouth, my fingers coated with desire.

I don't bother waiting for her to finish. I grab a condom from the bedside table, sheathe myself, and while she's still quivering, thrust my hard-on deep inside her. She's put on some weight in the months she's been eating well and being spoiled rotten by me, so her fuller tits and soft belly jiggle with every thrust. I love this version of Claire, maybe even more than any version. She's soft and full, happy and strong. Everything I always knew she could be.

I fuck her hard, the bed banging back and forth with my movements. She wraps her legs around my hips and lifts her ass to grind against me, greedily chasing another climax. I wait for it, cupping her ass and reaching between her cheeks to finger her asshole while she works her hips and begs for more.

When she finally comes again, I let go too, and we collapse against each other's naked bodies. We don't say anything, our sighs mingling, our bodies sweaty, until we both catch our breath.

"Better than coffee," Claire says with a grin.

"I still need at least one cup," I tell her.

"I'll make it," she says, and just then, we hear Aurora banging a toy against the wall.

"E!" she hollers from her room. "E!"

Claire looks at me and points at my chest. "She wants you. Smart girl." She leans over to kiss me. "I'll get coffee, you get the birthday girl."

Aurora's birthday was last week, and Claire and I

spent it alone. We wanted to celebrate the milestone as a family, the first of many, but one of the most important. Today is her big party, and we plan to treat her like the princess she is.

I throw on some clothes, stop to take a quick piss and rinse out my mouth, then I stand outside the door to the bedroom where Aurora sleeps. I knock on the door and call out to Aurora, playing her favorite morning game. "Aurora, are you up?"

"E," she squeals, and I hear her throw something at the door. It's how we play this little game.

"Aurora?" I call out again through the closed door. "Are you awake?"

"E!" She's squealing louder now, excited and revved up, knowing what comes next.

I push the door open a crack and peek at her with one eye. "I don't see you. Aurora, are you in here?"

"E!"

We play like this for about two more minutes, me picking up the plush toy she threw on the floor and asking the elephant if he knows where Aurora is. By the time Claire's got the coffee started, I've got Aurora in my arms and am planting loud raspberry kisses all over her neck.

I change her diaper—which, let me tell you, I only just started doing last week—and let her run around in the same PJs she slept in. Her mom's gonna bathe her and put on her special birthday party dress, so for now, we're going casual.

Once Aurora is changed, I take her little hand, and

she walks a few steps through the bedroom before losing patience with her nonexistent walking skills. She drops to her knees and fires off like a cannon, crawling into the living room.

"Mama," she calls.

Claire swoops her up and kisses her cheeks, then starts singing "Happy Birthday" to her.

I cover my ears, teasing Claire about her not-so-great singing voice. She tosses a couch pillow at me with a grin. "And because of that, you get to make the bed this morning."

I snort. It's always my job to make the bed in the morning. My phone pings, so I grab it and check the messages while I'm pouring a cup of coffee.

> Blade: You mind if I bring my kid? My plans for the afternoon kinda fell through.

I shake my head. Blade's protective of his son. I've never even met the kid. He's careful to keep his personal life personal.

> Me: Yeah, man, everybody's welcome. All Phantom's kids will be there. It's all good.

And that applies to every area of my life. Work has never been better.

Mad Dog got arrested coming back into the US on at least four outstanding warrants. He's locked up until his trials because nobody in the Hellfires would post bail. He's not gonna be a problem for us for a long time, if ever.

Shadow has taken on a leadership role on the business side. We have a dozen irons in the fire, and while I don't know what the future holds, I crack open a lot fewer heads these days, and I haven't taken a beating myself since I last tangled with Mad Dog.

Claire has a part-time job working for the city. The temp position got extended under a special contract, and while she's not yet making full-time money, she gets benefits for herself and the baby.

Poppy has gone back to work, so Claire and Poppy share a nanny. Three days a week, when Claire has to be in the office, she drops Aurora at Phantom's house, and their nanny watches Aurora and little Lilly.

I pour myself a cup of coffee and slice up a banana for the birthday girl. Claire is on the phone with one of her mom's friends—an old guy named Theo who used to play in Neon Dawn. She's been making friends and reconnecting with people from her life before Anthony.

As we move through the morning, I watch the woman I love and the baby I have come to adore. I've stopped setting aside as much money for my mom as I did before. I used to hoard the cash I made, thinking that I'd send it to Mom when she was old and sick and had no way to care for herself. I knew my old man wouldn't, and I never thought I'd be back in her life.

Now that I don't have to save up guilt money, I can think about what else I want to do with all the shit I've worked for over the last twelve years. I've more than made back what I spent to free Claire from the Hellfires. A house for my family might be in my future. We just bought Claire a car, and I've been dropping hints about a ring. But so far, we're just living it. Taking it day by blissful day.

When we get to Phantom's, he's got his shirt off, which, let me tell you, is not a sight I was prepared for. He's showing off the new ink he got for his newest daughter. "Holly, Daisy, Lilly," he says, proudly pointing to the design around his heart.

Poppy's son Jax narrows his eyes and pretends to glare at it. "That's not what I drew." He rolls his eyes. "Artistic license."

Phantom flicks the kid on the arm and gives him a wink. Those two are thick as thieves. Seeing Jax around the compound was weird at first. I avoided the nerdy kid who always had his nose in a drawing pad. But now that I have Aurora, I can see the appeal of a son. I don't get ahead of myself, though. I'm still getting used to the baby I have.

Speaking of which, I jostle Aurora in my arms and settle her on a hip. Claire brushes her bangs out of her eyes and follows a few steps behind me, holding on to the baby carrier just in case Aurora gets fussy or needs to lie down.

We barely make it inside Phantom's house before we're besieged by squealing teenage girls.

Holly and Daisy come skidding into the living room, their faces decorated with glitter. They have pink and purple glittery crowns on their heads, and they each have one in their hand. They're both wearing dresses and makeup and perfume, and it's like a roving cloud of happiness as they circle us with their hands out.

"Okay, okay, this one is for the birthday girl." Daisy takes charge, holding out her arms to take Aurora from me. I learned long ago not to fight the pull of a teenage girl who sets her sights on something. Besides, Aurora loves her babysitters and practically leaps out of my arms to get to Daisy.

"Whoa," I say. "Easy, Ror."

I set Aurora on the floor, and Daisy uses matching glitter hairpins to attach the crown to Aurora's hair. She has enough of it that the crown stays, but the look on her face tells me she's not sure whether to cry or like it because it's coming from some of her favorite people.

"Don't feel bad if she pulls it off," Claire says, a knowing grin on her face. "She's in a don't-touch-my-hair phase."

Daisy shakes her head. "I never went through one of those." Not a surprising statement since every time I see Daisy, some wildly unnatural color stripes through the front of her hair.

Holly is equally as excited to see Aurora, but she sidles up to Claire and loops an arm through hers. "Can you please distract my dad a little today? He's on fire about Corbin and me."

I look from Claire to Holly. "Who the fuck is Corbin?"

Daisy rolls her eyes and adjusts Aurora's crown. "Holly's flavor of the week," she says. "Since Dad won't let her date until she's eighteen, she has a lot of boy*friends*." She raises her brows dramatically, and I narrow my eyes.

"I'm with Phantom," I grit. "Where is this little prick of the week?"

"Savage." Claire grabs my arm and tugs me away, whispering something under her breath to Holly. "Let's go greet our hosts."

Holly blows Claire a kiss, and we leave the birthday girl with the teens. In the kitchen, Poppy is putting the finishing touches on the cupcakes. I don't know how she pulled this whole party off while already being back to work and having a four-month-old, but the woman is a star.

"Claire." Poppy turns from the stacks of pink-iced cupcakes and goes right to my woman. She folds her in a hard hug, and they rock back and forth even though they just saw each other literally four days ago. As soon as they release the hug, Poppy starts talking about a photo booth they got Tank to set up. I see the poor prospect out in the yard wearing a "The Birthday Girl Is My Boss" T-shirt and playing with what I can only assume is said photo booth. As the women rush past me toward the yard, Poppy kisses my cheek. "Oh, and hi to you, Savage."

I'm no Claire, but at least I merit a hello. I wander

outside with them, where Blade, Viper, Shadow, and Stella are chatting around a cooler. I grab a beer and look around the happy, festive scene.

I have to do a neck-wrenching double take when I see Phantom, his shirt back on, walking into the yard wearing their daughter Lilly in some kind of kangaroo wrap on his chest.

I lift a brow at him, and he grunts. "This was the only way to keep the girls from putting one of those damn crowns on the kid's head."

I snort, fully doubting that's the only reason he's wearing his kid on his chest. Something about having another daughter has loosened Phantom up even more when he's not at the compound. It's nice seeing him like this. It shows me what life could be possible for me and Claire and Aurora and whoever else belongs in our small family.

Jax, Poppy's son, and a bunch of his friends are swimming in Phantom's pool, and I see Holly and Corbin, or whoever he is, holding hands, while Daisy tries to help Aurora walk in her brand-new birthday sandals across the grass. I'll give it to Daisy. That glitter crown has made it more than ten minutes, which is ten more minutes than I predicted it would last.

I take a sip of my beer and look over my friends gathered together, when I feel Claire slip her hand into mine. "Come with me?" she says, asking it like a question.

I follow her back into the house, and we head toward the front door. Claire motions for me to open it.

When I open the door, I'm momentarily struck speechless, but the feeling wears off quickly. "Hey, Mom." I welcome Mom into Phantom's house with a hug.

She kisses my cheeks, then takes Claire in a long, warm embrace. "Thank you so, so much for inviting me." Mom's carrying a large gift bag, which I assume is for Aurora, and a gorgeous bouquet of flowers for Poppy.

This isn't the first time Mom has met the crew. Over the last six months, we've invited her here for a couple of cookouts. Neutral territory where we can chat and get to know each other again without the pressure of being alone.

As much as I want to rebuild a relationship with my mother, it's still raw. It's been probably the slowest part of my life to change in the last few months. But with all the other changes, I'd say reconnecting after twelve years is more than enough. We have, I hope, the rest of our lives to make up for lost time.

I won't go visit my old man, though. Mom and I have discussed it, and she is certain that my pops is in no shape to even recognize me. Without some kind of closure like I'm getting with my mom, I honestly think seeing my dad would only make things worse for me.

He's been dead to me for twelve years.

Some ghosts are better left in the ground.

Maybe I'll change my mind someday, but I doubt it.

Raising Aurora and having a child in my life has only made me angrier at him.

Every time I picture myself at Aurora's age, and I think of the way my dad treated me, with the hatred and violence, I know I'll never be able to forgive him. Not that he's capable of asking for it.

Mom, Poppy, and Claire talk with Violet in the kitchen while I keep an eye on Daisy and Aurora, all the while marveling at how they found a baby wrap big enough to fit Phantom's enormous torso.

We eat, sing happy birthday, open gifts, and I even bust Corbin twice for trying to sneak a kiss on Holly before Phantom sees a thing.

Blade's kid doesn't come after all. I don't know what happened, but Blade looks pretty shaken up. He's drinking more than I'd expect at a kids' party, but I don't pry. He's staring at Stella like she hung the moon.

I don't think she's interested in him, but like all of us, she's caring. Blade needs a woman who can fill the void left by his ex. I don't think Stella's that woman, but I'm glad he's got someone to talk to—especially when he's looking so low.

"Future looks bright, eh, man?" Shadow starts talking business, and by the time I realize how long we've been chatting, Claire slides underneath my arm.

"Excuse me for interrupting," she says, grinning at us. "But I'd like to pry our child away from Daisy and use that photo booth before it gets dark."

I lean down and kiss the top of her head, then lumber over to Daisy. "Urgent mission," I tell her. "Birthday pictures." I nod at Daisy, and she looks at me seriously.

"I'm on it," she says. She picks up Aurora and hands her to me, then tells me not to take any pics until she's back with a surprise.

I head over to the photo booth, where Claire is waiting. She wipes something off Aurora's cheek with a wet finger and smooths down her dress. Tank gives us the thumbs-up, but I tell him we're waiting for Daisy.

Daisy comes back with the world's most obscenely loud squeaky mouse. She squeezes it with her full strength, and Aurora laughs so hard, I can feel her fart in her diaper. Not cool, but also really cute.

"She loves this one," Daisy shouts over the squeaking. "Tank, take the pics."

Our little director shoots orders until Claire leans up to give me a kiss. Tank snaps a shot, and Daisy groans. "Old people kissing. I'm out."

Then she skips off toward the pool. I'm about to leave the photo setup when Claire holds my arm. "We need one more," she says. She asks Tank to wait, and then she trots off toward the kitchen. She comes back a minute later, holding my mom's elbow.

"Come on, Val," she says brightly. "Family photo."

Mom looks hesitantly toward me, and I extend my arms, offering her Aurora. Mom takes her, but her lower lip trembles and her eyes fill with tears. "Family photo," she echoes.

She tucks in between me and Claire, who wraps one arm around me, lowers her head to Val's shoulder, and keeps one hand on Aurora's shoulder.

"Say cheese!" Tank yells out.

"E!" Aurora yells, and just then, tears in our eyes and massive grins on our faces, Tank snaps the photo.

Our first birthday as a family.

And I know that now and forever, this, these people, will be my salvation.

Want more Hurricane Heat MC?
Hawk's book next and he's about to knock your socks off. To learn more and get your copy, please visit
menofinked.com/hawk

A SEXY MOTORCYCLE ROMANCE SERIES!
It's time to visit the OPEN ROAD.

Book 1 - Broken Sparrow (Morris)
Book 2 - Broken Dove (Leo)
Book 3 - Broken Wings (Crow)
Book 4 - Broken Arrow (Arrow)
Book 5 - Broken Hearts (Eagle)

Also available in discreet paperbacks

Learn more by visiting
menofinked.com/open-road-series

♥ Men of Inked Reader Guide ♥

DOWNLOAD NOW

*Visit **menofinked.com/guide** to grab the extensive Chelle Bliss Reading Guide, which includes a family tree, printable guide, and information about the Gallo family saga.*

BECOME A MEMBER OF THE FAMILY...

Want a place to talk romance books, meet other bookworms, and all things Men of Inked? Join Chelle Bliss Books on Facebook to get sneak peeks, exclusive news, and special giveaways.

Want to be the first to hear about the next Men of Inked book or everything Chelle Bliss? Join my newsletter by visiting _menofinked.com/inked-news_ or scan the QR code below.

LOVE AUDIOBOOKS?

All audiobooks are only $4.99!

<u>Tap here to learn more</u> or visit *chelleblissromance.com*

ABOUT THE AUTHOR

I'm a full-time writer, time-waster extraordinaire, social media addict, coffee fiend, and ex-history teacher. *To learn more about my books, please visit menofinked.com.*

Want to stay up-to-date on the newest Men of Inked release and more? [Tap here to join my newsletter](#) or visit *menofinked.com/inked-news*

Join over 10,000 readers on Facebook in [Chelle Bliss Books](#) private reader group and talk books and all things reading. [Tap here to become part of the family](#) or visit at *facebook.com/groups/blisshangout*

[Tap here to see the Gallo Family Tree](#) or visit *menofinked.com/gallo-family-tree*

Where to Follow Me:

- facebook.com/authorchellebliss1
- instagram.com/authorchellebliss
- bookbub.com/authors/chelle-bliss
- goodreads.com/chellebliss
- amazon.com/author/chellebliss
- tiktok.com/@chellblissauthor
- pinterest.com/chellebliss10

LOVE SIGNED PAPERBACKS & SPECIAL EDITIONS?

Visit *chelleblissromance.com* for signed paperbacks and book merchandise.

www.ingramcontent.com/pod-product-compliance
Lightning Source LLC
LaVergne TN
LVHW031541060526
838200LV00056B/4598